"I'm not Juno Monroyale."

"What?" While Alvaro's eyes widened, their focus was laser-like.

"I'm her sister."

"You're not Juno." He stared so hard he paralyzed her. "If you're not Juno..."

She was Jade. She was the queen of Monrova.

Confessions were supposed to relieve—instead desolation slid deep, painfully filling hidden cuts, as she watched him make the connection.

"If you're not Juno," he said harshly, "then I'm not your boss."

He suddenly stepped forward and that desolation was swept away by a tsunami of something so much hotter. So much more that she couldn't think to answer.

"I'm not your boss," he repeated angrily, almost to himself.

And she realized that he'd just let something within himself go.

His hand hit her waist in a firm, heavy hold that made her heart thud. She couldn't tear her gaze from his—couldn't move, or speak. Her lips parted, yet she still couldn't breathe as an enormous wave of want tumbled over her again, drenching her with a desire so powerful it knocked over any hesitation, any caution, any reality. All she could hear was her heated blood beating, all she wanted was the touch she'd craved for days.

Just a taste.

The Christmas Princess Swap

It's the season for scandal!

Separated by a bitter divorce, when identical twin princesses Juno and Jade are finally reunited, they are overjoyed. And intrigued... A month in each other's shoes might be the perfect solution to both of their problems! What's the worst that can happen? Yet soon the sisters are embroiled in a Christmas scandal of truly royal proportions...!

Juno may have escaped the media scandal she caused back in NYC, but how will she tame the heat King Leonardo stirs inside her?

Find out in
The Royal Pregnancy Test
by Heidi Rice

Dutiful Jade needs a break from her royal life, but she never expected sparks to fly with Juno's billionaire boss, Alvaro Byrne.

Discover more in
The Queen's Impossible Boss
by Natalie Anderson

Don't miss this sparkling festive duet!

Natalie Anderson

—

THE QUEEN'S
IMPOSSIBLE BOSS

HARLEQUIN
PRESENTS

Recycling programs
for this product may
not exist in your area.

ISBN-13: 978-1-335-89424-3

The Queen's Impossible Boss

Copyright © 2020 by Natalie Anderson

This edition published by arrangement with Harlequin Books S.A.

For questions and comments about the quality of this book,
please contact us at CustomerService@Harlequin.com.

Harlequin Enterprises ULC
22 Adelaide St. West, 40th Floor
Toronto, Ontario M5H 4E3, Canada
www.Harlequin.com

Printed in U.S.A.

USA TODAY bestselling author **Natalie Anderson** writes emotional contemporary romance full of sparkling banter, sizzling heat and uplifting endings—perfect for readers who love to escape with empowered heroines and arrogant alphas who are too sexy for their own good. When she's not writing, you'll find Natalie wrangling her four children, three cats, two goldfish and one dog... and snuggled in a heap on the sofa with her husband at the end of the day. Follow her at natalie-anderson.com.

Books by Natalie Anderson

Harlequin Presents

The Forgotten Gallo Bride
Claiming His Convenient Fiancée
The King's Captive Virgin
Awakening His Innocent Cinderella
Pregnant by the Commanding Greek
The Greek's One-Night Heir
Secrets Made in Paradise

Conveniently Wed!

The Innocent's Emergency Wedding

Once Upon a Temptation

Shy Queen in the Royal Spotlight

One Night With Consequences

Princess's Pregnancy Secret

Visit the Author Profile page
at Harlequin.com for more titles.

For my Bubble

Thank you for being so supportive and patient while I wrote this when we were all holed up together—the apple sponges were amazing!

CHAPTER ONE

'GIVEN YOU'VE NOT BOTHERED to reply to any earlier messages, don't bother coming back at all.'

Jade Monroyale shivered as that stern dismissal echoed in her head, but for once in her life she was going to disobey a direct order. She strode along the Manhattan pavement in her travel-stale clothes, masking her nerves as she wheeled the one small suitcase she'd been able to bring with her. The number of people heading to work was amazing, given it was still very early and so cold her fingers and toes were numb. She'd have loved a hot shower, but, having heard that message only an hour ago, she'd known she had no time to waste. She had to get to the office and fix things.

'Don't bother.'

His low tone had been underlined by an edge of danger. Authoritative and uncompromising, his anger had been barely leashed. Jade knew that kind of man well—impatient, dismissive, arrogant. But there'd been another frisson in his voice—a passion that had alarmed her more than the accusation had.

Navigating the subway had been something else. She'd run her sister's MetroCard the wrong way a few times before figuring it out. Swiping cards through machines ought to be something anyone could do but, as Queen of a prosperous, albeit small, European country, Jade Monroyale had never carried either cash or cards before. Her father had deemed it unnecessary given destiny dictated her future. She was 'different', she had a 'rare duty'…and he'd ensured she never forgot it. But now she felt a very different duty. Her twin needed her help.

'Juno? This is Alvaro Byrne.'

He'd introduced himself brusquely as he'd left the last of the many messages on Juno's phone. A couple of workmates and her immediate manager had left several, but Alvaro Byrne—the CEO himself—had left just that last one.

Juno, Jade's younger sister by a mere two minutes, had lived here in New York for more than a decade, the identical twins separated by much more than their parents' traumatic divorce. But for the first time Jade was in a position to be able to help Juno. She was not having her sister's job lost because of a lapse in communication. Her twin hadn't been able to respond to those calls because she'd been travelling. She hadn't even *heard* them. Jade was so glad Juno didn't understand the degree to which her job was in peril. And if Jade could finesse it, she need never know. All Jade had to do was pull off this impersonation to perfection...

Yes, their twin switch was *crazy*—especially considering they'd not been together for years and knew so little of each other's daily lives—but it was worth the risk. Juno desperately needed time in Monrova. While Jade?

Finally, for just a few weeks, she'd be free.

Until last night, Jade had barely left her home. As she was the only heir her father had acknowledged in recent years, there could be no risk of them both being in an accident. So they'd never travelled together. Jade had been strictly limited in where she could go, what she could do. Her entire life had been spent preparing for the role she was destined to fulfil. She'd studied several languages, history, geography, absorbed political and diplomatic theory, mastered manners and etiquette and, most of all, emotional control. She'd learned never to let fear or hurt or anger show—for, according to her father, a monarch must remain impassive in public. That was absolute.

Pretty ironic given that, behind that pretty palace facade, her parents' separation had been so acrimonious and bitter that they'd forced Jade and Juno apart when they were only eight. Jade, as firstborn, had remained with her father to be groomed as future Queen, while Juno had been sent to the United States with her mother. It was a decision Jade still struggled to forgive, even all these years later. She'd been forbidden to see her mother again. And their authoritarian father had disapproved of their mother's more permissive parenting style and the defiance that an independent Juno wasn't afraid to display when she was allowed to visit for holidays that were too brief. Finally, in the summer in which they'd turned sixteen, Juno had stormed from their father's autocratic displeasure in Monrova, never to return.

'I expect my employees to be team players and to value their colleagues.'

Alvaro Byrne's stinging rebuke had stopped Jade in her tracks. Juno had suffered enough thanks to one unforgiving man, Jade wasn't letting it happen again. Especially not for something so minor. *No one* was as loyal as Juno, and this jerk hadn't even given her the chance to explain.

In the past Jade's only act of defiance had been to stay in touch with Juno after that last fight, despite her father's ever-looming disapproval. A month before they'd turned eighteen their mother had passed, leaving Juno alone and isolated miles away. Jade had been prevented from going to the funeral and unable to offer any real comfort and Juno had made it clear she had no desire to return to Monrova. Jade had learned to bypass the Internet security wall that had previously stopped her from seeing her sister's social media postings and they'd video conferenced when they could. Juno had regaled her with tales of her life as the media-dubbed 'Rebel Princess' in New York…

But Juno still hadn't come back when their father had died just a year ago. And while her choice had saddened Jade, she'd understood that some things were so painful they were impossible to overcome…or at least, took a long, long time. So Juno's surprise visit to Monrova at the weekend had been the best thing ever. And her suggestion of a three-week twin-switch?

Yes, it absolutely was crazy. But Juno needed time in her own country—she needed time to understand the heritage and the life that had been denied her.

And yes, there was a selfish element to Jade's ready agreement. For Jade to have just a little time to herself and live like a 'normal' person with relative anonymity? To experience a few of those freedoms that only a city like New York could offer? To have time to herself before fulfilling her late father's last wish? And Christmas—an actual special, even if alone, Christmas. She'd barely been able to admit it even to herself, but the chance to experience life a little more 'normal' had been irresistible.

'How could you just ignore their calls?'

There was that emotive edge in Alvaro Byrne's tone that had scalded Jade. It seemed her 'little more normal' now included dealing with

Juno's irate boss at work. She was determined to defuse this situation. Duty—responsibility—was everything and right now she was responsible for Juno's reputation.

Jade had her own challenging choice ahead. She would do anything for her country—even marry the man her father had decided would be the best match for her politically. Since his death, her advisors had unanimously insisted that the marriage was still the best course of action for both Monrova and for Queen Jade herself. If it *was*, then of course she would do it. But Juno had been horrified that Jade was even considering marriage to King Leonardo of Severene—the neighbouring nation—and she'd wanted to give Jade space to consider everything. Juno had handed over her phone, passport, passwords...and Jade had been swept along by her twin's insistence and enthusiastic assurance that they could pull this off.

Because she'd not just wanted it, she'd needed it too.

But Juno had said there was no need for Jade to go into her work as she could work from home in this last week before the office closed early for the Christmas break, lessening the chances of someone suspecting their switch. Only when Jade had landed at the airport in New York and turned on Juno's phone, it had pinged incessantly, signalling an insane amount of messages and voicemails.

And this last—from the CEO himself—was the one that spurred Jade's action now.

'This is Alvaro Byrne.'

He was CEO of a conglomerate that had started with an eclectic suite of popular apps and mushroomed since to include both property and financial investments. Juno had been recruited to work in the social media marketing arm for the suite of apps, including that original fitness tracking one—Byrne IT. Juno had mentioned a minor issue at work in passing, but when Jade had looked online after hearing those messages, she saw the fuss was more major than Juno had realised and it was only escalating.

On her journey in from the airport, Jade had searched online for any information she could find about the office and her co-workers but there'd been little about the structure. So she'd listened again to the catalogue of increasingly concerned voice messages and memorised the names of the callers—grateful for the disciplined memory techniques drilled into her from a young age. Then she'd coiled her hair into a bun to hide the fact that hers was longer and straighter than Juno's and hoped that her plain black trousers and white shirt were suitably 'Juno office wear'. She figured her black coat covered much anyway, and if she could somehow fix this quickly, she could be out of there before the others arrived for the day.

Finally, at Byrne HQ, in Tribeca, she stared

through the gleaming glass to the brightly lit, funky atrium of the repurposed brick-fronted industrial building. She shuffled through Juno's battered wallet to find the office security card. To her relief the door lock clicked when she swiped it through the security pad. So Juno hadn't been banned from the building, despite the unreasonable rancour in that man's tone.

She quickly read the signs and ventured deeper into the quiet building. She shivered again, nerves biting. But she had no choice but to ignore their agreement for her to stay away from Juno's work. She had to fix it so everything would be well when Juno returned. She knew this job mattered to her sister—she'd shut down the social media sites she'd been running for years because she'd wanted to pull back from that public 'Rebel Princess' persona. She'd wanted a normal marketing job for a company and to get some anonymity back. So, more than anything, Jade wanted to help her sister keep it.

Those two minutes that separated them as 'heir' and 'spare' were merely fate, but Jade hated that Juno had effectively been ejected from the kingdom. She knew her father's hard-line stance stemmed from a deep, devastated hurt, but that didn't make it okay. And Jade had been too scared to challenge her father on it. Too scared that if she too hurt him, or let him down in some way as her mother had, then she too would be rejected. She'd tried for years to be the perfect princess daughter. Now she had the chance to be a decent sister.

She took the elevator to the sixth floor, grateful for the clear signs. There was a large open-plan area with several desks in groups, separated by a couple of sofas, and a number of glass-walled offices ran along the side. How was she meant to know which was Juno's desk? She paused, taking in the personal items on each one in the hope she might find a clue. Then she spotted an enormous hot pink coffee mug with *Princess* emblazoned on the side. Jade smiled the second she saw it, her amusement bubbling up. That 'own it' attitude was pure Juno. She wheeled her cabin bag up to the desk, shrugged out of her coat, hung it on the back of the swivel chair and eyed up the computer. All she needed to do now was get online, get a few messages and emails sent and she'd be out of here.

'What do you think you're doing?'

Jade wasn't listening to that icy but irate phone message now, but there was no mistaking that voice. She instantly swung round, drawing in a breath to reply—but then she choked.

'Oh.' She gulped, staggered by the sight before her.

First impression? Skin. Second impression? Muscles. Third? Fury—in the heated tension in his tight stance. All of it up close and personal and towering over her.

Jade suddenly felt as if she were being incinerated from the inside out. Awareness—purely, *mortifyingly*, sexual—swamped her, frying her brain. He was huge. Like really, *really* tall and muscular in a way she wasn't used to.

Of course, she wasn't used to it.

The man was gleaming and hot—literally. She could almost see the steam rising from his body. Why—*why*—was his chest bare? Finally—far too late—she dragged her gaze up from his abs and pecs, past his wide shoulders to the tanned column of his neck, his sharp-edged jaw, grim-set mouth and then there, to the blazing anger in his amber eyes.

'Juno, right?' he said tightly. 'You need to leave.'

This wasn't the setting for so much skin. That was why she was reacting so primally, right? Frankly she wasn't used to seeing half-naked men, *ever*. No matter that it was an office situation, not in *any* situation was she used to this.

'You're...' she trailed off, forced to swallow in an attempt to ease her dry throat.

'Still wondering why you're here,' he snapped.

Couldn't the same be said for him? It was ridiculously early and what was he doing here *barely dressed*? Black sports shorts and trainers were all he had on.

Alvaro Byrne.

Tall, dark and wild. Even his hair was a little long and now he swept it out of his eyes with an impatient hand. The already tense muscles in his chest rippled.

'Why are you here?' he demanded. 'Didn't you get my message?'

'I—'

'Don't need to be here. Leave. Now.'

Seriously? He wasn't even going to listen to her? Wasn't going to take a breath? 'No. I'm here to—'

'Why aren't you moving?'

'Why aren't *you* listening?'

He folded his arms in front of her. The stance just made his biceps pop more.

Jade, who'd held her nerve for so many years, in so many public situations in Monrova, was completely distracted. For the first time ever, her brain slipped into mush territory and her tongue slipped away from her.

'You...' It wasn't good enough. She needed to do better for Juno. She drew a deep breath and began again. 'You need to give me a chance.'

'You've had plenty of chances. But you haven't answered any calls or messages for forty-eight hours. And now you walk in here looking...'

Jade tensed warily. Looking what? Had he guessed already?

'Like butter wouldn't melt,' he finished with a growl.

She was buffeted by a wave of relief that she might pull this off. He hadn't instantly recognised that she wasn't Juno. She struggled to stare calmly back at him. Never had it been so hard to stand still and stay cool.

'Forty-eight hours, Juno,' he repeated. 'Why didn't you return any calls?'

It was always best to answer with honesty, right? Or at least with as much honesty as she was able at this point in time. 'I was out of range.'

'Really? That's what you're going with?' He couldn't look more disbelieving. 'Maybe you should have stayed out of range.'

'I'm here now.'

'Why?'

'Why do you think?'

'What do you think you can possibly do to make this better?'

She had no idea. Never had she been challenged with such hostility or fury and she was lost for words.

His eyebrows lifted. 'Way too little, way too late.'

Jade was tired from the flight. Stressed from maintaining a stupid lie for such a short time already. This had been such a bad idea. The little 'snafu' that Juno had mentioned had apparently morphed into something bigger. But this—creature—couldn't be that unreasonable. And she needed to re-engage her brain. 'I couldn't...'

'I'm going to shower and dress,' he interrupted, apparently bored already. 'You'll be gone when I return.'

He'd turned his back on her and was walking away before she could blink.

Jade gaped as she watched him stride through the office. He thought he could just fire her? Be that dismissive? He hadn't even given her a chance to properly explain, let alone offer a solution. Never had she met someone so unreasonable.

She'd bitten off more than she could chew. She'd been impetuous and foolish and she had no way of pulling this off. But this was for Juno and she had to succeed at saving her sister's job. She was *not* giving up.

Alvaro strode through the office to the bathroom and flicked the shower to cold, desperate to regain control over the appallingly base reaction of his body. That woman had walked in here at stupidly early o'clock—wheeling a case, for some strange reason—and frankly almost looking furtive. He'd finished his workout only five minutes earlier and followed her progress from his office. He'd seen her smile as she'd made her way to her desk. A smile of pure joy. Why was she so amused by this situation?

And worse was that *he'd* been flooded with a heat that was outrageous in its intensity. Anger, right?

Not entirely.

But that visceral betrayal of his body had only exacerbated his anger. He refused to be physically attracted to Juno Monroyale. Hell, he barely knew her. His marketing manager had pitched hiring her to him only a few weeks ago, but he'd been overseas setting up a major deal and hadn't spent much time in the office since her arrival.

Unfortunately, it turned out that the princess was stunning. Her eyes a gorgeous, bewitching green. Her brunette hair was swept up in a high bun that emphasised cheekbones and plump lips and her pretty little chin tempted him to tilt it upwards so she could take his kiss.

It was appalling. He'd not been paralysed by lust like this in quite a while. Not as instantly or as intensely or as inappropriately. She was an employee. Worse, she was an employee who'd screwed up. *Royally.*

So the sooner she was out of here, the better.

He glared at the shower wall as if his eyes were lasers and could burn right through the tile and wood to where that woman was wheeling her damn case out of here.

She'd *better* be walking out of here—in those thin-soled stupid shoes with their little high heels that were useless for the snow-threatened streets of New York. It said it all, right? Ill-equipped for real life? She was a literal princess who didn't own up to her mistakes. She'd apparently abandoned her colleagues—did she just assume that someone else would clear up the mess?

He knew too well how that worked. He knew

people with such privilege who'd refused to carry the burdens of their own responsibility—their own *mistakes*. His own 'family' were the perfect example of that—while he'd been the 'mistake'.

So he had little time to sympathise with Her Royal Highness. And he had little time to get this sorted. But he would, because *he'd* built this entire company—with determined, round-the-clock effort. Its increasing success had meant he'd had to assemble teams around him, but at heart he preferred independence and self-reliance. He'd never liked asking anyone to help him. Never expected anyone would—not unless there was something in it for themselves. Something like a fat pay cheque.

This princess had no idea what building this success had taken. Whether her cluelessness was based in pure entitled privilege, or mere carelessness, it didn't matter. Whichever it was, he didn't want her around.

To be honest, it wasn't the actual social media post he was bothered about. While that app was his oldest and he had a soft spot for it, it wasn't his core business now. But it was the *trust* that had been damaged. And he was in the middle of a delicate acquisition and the last thing he needed was for his prospective target to be frightened off.

He exited the shower and dressed, yanking a shirt from the hanger and swiftly buttoning it. Then he strode back out to the office to check that she'd obeyed his order and had gone.

She hadn't.

He paused a few paces away from where she sat at her desk, focusing hard on the computer screen before her. 'Why are you still here?'

She didn't stop typing. 'Because I'm sorting out this issue.'

'The only issue here is that you haven't left yet,' he scoffed.

'Then call your security, I'm not leaving.' She spun her seat round a few inches and glared up at him.

Oh, really? Adrenalin rippled within him at her audible defiance. 'I don't need security to help haul your ass out of this building. I can scoop you up with one hand.' In fact, both of his hands were itching right now.

'Try it and see how far you get,' she snapped back.

Jade never snapped. Ever. And to her absolute amazement, she just had. Their gazes clashed. Never had she felt as small as she did sitting on this chair, nor had she felt such appalling anticipation.

'Not going to give you the thrill,' he muttered through clenched teeth.

'Not going to move,' she replied.

She'd laid the challenge with loathing, but a second later a wave of longing swept over her. She *wanted* to feel his hands grab her waist and haul her to her feet and press her against his hard body. She wanted it so intensely, with such ferocity that for a second, as she stared into his eyes, she actually believed that *he* wanted it too. That he envisioned exactly that—the two of them pressed tightly together.

Her heart thudded as they silently squared off. Impossibly, he was more dangerous now in that sharp white shirt and the black trousers. She could sense the heat and strength of the muscles she knew full well were primed beneath that expensive fabric. But she refused to flinch, or shrink back...right now she refused to even breathe.

He still just stared at her. But where his stance was furious, his eyes were nothing but warm— a honeyed amber iris and melting, deep pupils that widened the more she watched—daring her nearer, willing her to dive in and drown.

'Let me have a go at fixing this,' she eventually croaked.

'And make it worse?'

'Why not trust me to do the job I was hired to do?'

'You've already shown you're incapable of doing that. You chose to walk out.'

'So a person can't make a single mistake? You can't give someone a second chance? This wasn't a capital offence, Alvaro. This wasn't even *illegal*.'

It had been the tiniest mistake and he was totally overreacting.

'It was a data breach.'

'Actually, it wasn't,' she said firmly. 'It clearly states in the terms and conditions of the app that Byrne IT has the right to use that data in any publicity.'

His gaze narrowed on her.

Yes, she'd spent the time waiting for the train reading up all she could. And she was good at reading long, boring documents and legalese.

'While it wasn't ideal and while it certainly might not have been best policy,' she continued, 'it *wasn't* illegal. And you can change the policy to better reflect what your consumers are now saying they want.'

'You're not going to admit to doing anything wrong?'

'Actually, the contrary.' She straightened on her chair—pointless as it was because he was still so much taller than her. 'I take full responsibility. It was *my* mistake and I'll apologise for it.'

Juno had posted the wrong graphic on one of their social media channels. Version one instead of version two. Version one included user names whereas version two had been made anonymous. It had been such a simple mistake but some of those users had noticed and didn't like their user-names being displayed. The lack of initial response had led to that small flame of discontent flaring to a dumpster blaze and an online debate about privacy rights.

'Fine. You've apologised. Now you can leave.'

'Not leaving.' She spun back to the screen.

'What are you doing?'

She didn't glance away from the computer. 'I said I'd apologise.'

'You just did.'

'Not only to you.'

He paused. 'You're emailing the team before you leave?'

'I already have. Because I'm sorry for going AWOL at the weekend, but I'm back. And now I'm replying to the complainants.'

'What?'

'*Everyone* makes mistakes,' she said heatedly. 'And most people deserve a second chance, right?' she said. 'Most *normal* people are willing to give that.' She sent him a look.

He folded his arms across his very muscular chest. 'You think a little apology is going to make this all go away?'

'An acknowledgement can mean a lot.' She nodded.

'As can getting something for free,' he added cynically.

'Then I'll give them a month free on their subscription. You can take it directly from my salary.' She swallowed. She could cover that cost for Juno once she was back in Monrova. And it would be worth it just to prove herself in front of the furious one here.

'You're willing to the pay the price all by yourself?' he asked.

She glanced back and looked directly into those heart-stopping eyes. 'I'm willing to do whatever it takes.'

'I didn't think royals were known for admission of any kind of guilt,' he commented acidly.

Oh, so he had a thing against all royals? Not just Juno in particular? 'Did you think we're all spoilt and entitled?'

'I think…' He paused, his words coming soft but dangerous nonetheless. 'I think you need to prove yourself, Princess.'

She looked at him a moment longer and then lifted her chin. 'Fine,' she breathed, bluffing as best she could. 'No problem.'

CHAPTER TWO

No problem?

The annoying thing was, that appeared to be the case. Three hours into it, Alvaro studied the princess from the relative privacy of his office. She looked pale and thinner—at least he thought she did. Truthfully, he'd not spent much time considering her as he'd been away working on a deal. But Juno was right, this wasn't a 'data breach' and they hadn't actually contravened their own privacy policy, and perhaps her suggestion they amend their terms was worth considering.

So now he watched her messages appear online with interest. She was responding to every comment already made, signing each one 'PJ'.

I'm sorry for the error. It was entirely my mistake. This was your story to share.

To his amazement, the diffusion of emotion was happening before his eyes. Comments kept appearing—more, then more replies to her responses. Now people were telling her not to worry about it? People were feeling sorry that she'd made a mistake? How had she got them onside so quickly?

Everyone makes mistakes, but mine impacted directly on you. I can only apologise and thank you for accepting my apology.

She'd written to one formerly cross customer and now they were asking her which was her favourite workout and chatting like old friends?

He looked up to observe her again. She was almost smiling as she typed—a whisper of a sweet smile. He'd had his doubts about hiring her, cynically thinking that his marketing manager just wanted to sprinkle some quasi-celebrity glitter about the place. And that Juno was cynical too, only doing this for profit. Prior to this she'd been an 'influencer' or something—he'd assumed that meant she merely peddled whatever product people would give her just to make a buck.

But maybe he'd been wrong about that, because she was genuinely engaged and actually enjoying this interaction. She worked quickly, using two computers to check on different social media channels, answering comments as quickly as she could. But the comments were snowballing now. One made him flinch. It was personally abusive. *Vile.*

Instinctively he stood, but before he could move

she'd posted a polite, finite response. And now others had boosted her response and, in only moments, the abusive comment was buried in an avalanche of support for the princess.

So why had she skipped out for the weekend, then? Why hadn't she replied to any of those messages from her workmates? No one had heard from her. No one had been able to reach her. Sophy, her direct manager, had been stressed—now Alvaro buzzed for them both.

'Sophy, can you help Juno moderate those comments?' he said shortly when they appeared in his doorway. 'She shouldn't have to see some of those…'

'I can handle them,' Juno replied before Sophy had the chance. 'They're only words and this shouldn't impact on anyone else's workload any more than it already has.'

Alvaro stared, his breath stolen by her restrained dignity—so different from the flare he'd seen from her this morning. 'Are you sure?'

She nodded.

Through the afternoon he drank another two coffees and kept an eye on Juno. She didn't move from her chair for hours. Surely, she needed food or a bathroom break? She'd didn't stop to chat to colleagues much either. On the socials, there were more comments than ever. But not angry ones. Somehow, she'd got people sharing stories about when they'd screwed up. The community was more active than it had been in ages.

'We've had a bump in sign-ups today.' Sophy reappeared in his doorway, looking smug. 'Across all the apps. They love her response and her apologies. She's given us a masterclass in social media management,' Sophy added. 'Talk about the power of authenticity. And somehow she's done it in a way that hasn't made her a martyr.'

Alvaro didn't respond. He was facing the discomforting fact that he wasn't going to be able to fire her now. It ought to be good to have someone with such expert social media skills on his team. So why did he feel thwarted? And what was with this prickling sense of danger?

He clamped down on the obvious reason. He refused to acknowledge the heat that had hit the second he'd clashed with her at five o'clock this morning.

'They want to talk to her.' Sophy turned and watched Juno from his office. 'They like being able to talk to a real princess.'

He stiffened, bothered by that being the reason for her success. Were they *using* her because of who she was? He didn't feel comfortable that he was benefitting in some way because of the name she had and the family she'd been born into. That he was taking advantage of something that was beyond her control…

And yet it wasn't beyond her control. *She* was

the one out there commenting, choosing how to respond, choosing to take the time. She could have chosen not to come back at all. She could have left when he'd told her to first thing this morning. But she hadn't.

Then again, perhaps that was because she *needed* this job, needed to utilise whatever skills or assets or abilities she had—ones she was born with every bit as much as the ones she'd developed. Just because she was a princess, didn't mean she had everything.

He knew what it was like having to do whatever it took to survive—sucking up crap jobs or working all hours. His foster carer, Ellen, had done that, taught him through her example that work ethic was everything. The one thing you could control.

So all he could do was respect and appreciate Juno's effort and dignity. Yet he remained uncomfortable. He hadn't felt this wary in years—not since that dreadful day when he was nine years old and had been dragged to face his biological 'family' only to be rejected all over again. And then abandoned. Again.

'We need to clarify those terms and conditions,' he said to Sophy irritably. 'Get legal on it for me.'

'Sure thing.' But Sophy didn't leave. 'One of the online news bulletins has requested to interview you and Juno—she'd be good—'

'Juno's busy,' he said decisively. 'I'll handle it.'

He wasn't using her more today. Furthermore, he needed to get his inappropriate attraction under control. What was with *that* landing on him today? Why when he'd barely noticed her before now?

Maybe he was coming down with some kind of fever because within one second of seeing her this morning, he'd been burning up and hadn't cooled since.

She was still responding to that online chaos. Incredibly focused and calm. Too calm. Had he imagined that fiery argument from her this morning? Irritated, he stood to escape the office for a breather.

'You sound different today, Juno,' one assistant mused.

'I was with some people from Monrova over the weekend,' Juno answered. But as Alvaro passed her she saw him and a slow flush clouded across her pale cheeks. 'My accent always becomes stronger then...'

He tore his gaze from hers and strode out of the office. He barely managed to maintain his smile through the interview as her words from this morning rang in his ears.

'Everyone makes mistakes and most people deserve a second chance, right?'

Exhausted and stiff, Jade tilted her head to stretch out the tension in her neck and shoulders.

'Why are you still here?'

Surely, he didn't mean that? Her heart thudded as she spun once more to face the penetrating amber eyes of Alvaro Byrne. She'd been waiting for hours for him to return from that wretched online interview she'd watched, fiddling with the computer system and avoiding talking too much to Juno's colleagues before they finished for the day and left her alone.

'I'm glad you agree everyone makes mistakes,' she said quietly. 'And that everyone deserves a second chance.'

'You saw the interview?' His lips twisted. 'You argued compellingly—are you not pleased I took your thoughts on board?'

Jade was too tired to be left in any doubt. 'Does everyone include me?'

His gaze softened. 'I'm not afraid to admit when I'm wrong either, Juno. I appreciate everything you've done today.'

But she shrank, because him calling her 'Juno' made her feel guiltier than ever.

His jaw tightened. 'Look, you weren't to know, but I've been away working on a sensitive deal,' he said. 'I didn't react well this morning and I apologise for that.'

Oh. His quiet apology almost broke her last defences.

'I know it looked like I'd just walked out...' She drew breath, determined to be as honest as possible while still protecting Juno. 'There was something I had to attend to at the weekend. I'm sorry I wasn't in touch sooner.'

He gazed at her, too still, too intent, for her comfort.

'Sophy said that before this happened you'd planned to take leave from work this week?'

She nodded warily.

'Would you mind coming into the office instead? I'd appreciate your input on a couple of project streams and I think the team could benefit from your expertise. Unless you have plans you can't change?'

'Um—I…' This nightmare was going from bad to worse, yet she couldn't seem to say 'no' to him. 'Of course, I can come in.'

Ordinarily she could maintain a calm facade better than anyone. Ordinarily she would never say 'um'…but at this moment in front of Alvaro Byrne, she was a breath away from falling apart.

'That's great. Thank you.' Though he didn't look all that thrilled. 'But for now, it's late and you've had a long day. How are you getting home?'

Jade had no idea how to answer him. She didn't even know where home was. She had gone into this without properly thinking it through. Too late she'd realised the utter stupidity of her decision to come into the office this morning. Because while she'd secured Juno's job today, she was probably going to lose it for her tomorrow. She couldn't possibly keep this up. And she certainly couldn't cope with the hot bomb that was Alvaro Byrne.

'You shouldn't go on public transport this time of night.' He frowned.

'I can manage,' she lied.

'Just humour me,' he growled. 'You've gone above and beyond and been here hours. The least I can do is ensure you get home safely. I'll call a car.'

'I don't need—'

His gaze narrowed again. 'Company expense, Juno.'

She *really* didn't like him calling her by that name. But she couldn't tell him not to.

The easiest thing to do right now ought to be to say yes, to stop arguing with him. Except oddly it was the hardest task she'd faced all day. Drawing on that mantle of polite courtesy that had been drilled into her from birth was almost impossible.

'Thank you,' she finally said. 'That would be wonderful.'

'Wonderful?' He stared at her for a long moment.

Jade had the sudden suspicion she'd inadvertently jumped from the frying pan to the fire.

'Oh, sure,' he muttered softly but so dryly she nearly shivered. 'Let's call it wonderful.'

CHAPTER THREE

JADE SHRUGGED ON her jacket, extended the handle of her cabin bag and followed Alvaro to the elevator.

'You really were out of range?' He glanced at her bag as he pushed the buttons.

'I really was.' To her relief, he didn't ask for any more detail.

She was hugely relieved at the prospect of a car taking her straight home too. All she had to do then was unlock Juno's apartment. She was so tired she might fall into bed fully dressed.

She exited the lift ahead of him, increasingly desperate to escape his company. He was too tall, too intense, too magnetic and she was too aware of his every movement.

A sleek black sports car was parked right outside the building. The kind of low-slung roadster, capable of lethal speed, that her father and her protection officers would never let her near. To her horror, Alvaro walked around to the driver's door and got in. When she didn't move, the passenger window glided down.

'Come on.'

'I thought you said you called a car,' she said stupidly.

'I did. My car. The building valet brought it to the front for me.'

She'd thought he'd meant a taxi.

'You're driving me home?' Her audible breathlessness made her wince. If only she could instantly shrivel to ant size. The thought of having to spend more time with him ought to be terrifying, but her suddenly sprinting pulse was actually due to *excitement*. So awkward. And that restless ache inside was so wrong. She stared at the car and then back at him and tried not to melt in the warm amber of his eyes.

There was a long pause.

'You know you're not at risk from me,' he finally muttered. 'I'm not in the habit of harassing my employees.'

And now she was beyond mortified. 'I didn't think that you were.'

'So take this as all that it is, an apology and a small service to show my appreciation for your extra effort today. But if you would prefer I get a driver—'

'No, please don't,' she said hurriedly. 'I was just surprised. You've had a long day too.' She climbed into the car and fastened the belt and resolutely stared ahead.

'If you say the address the navigation will pick it up,' he said blandly.

Relieved, Jade parroted the address she'd memorised and sat back as the automated instruction began. The car silently glided along and she realised it had an electric engine. As she relaxed into the comfortable seat, tiredness swept over her. She could hardly keep her eyes open, only then—

'Is that your stomach rumbling?' Alvaro laughingly glanced at her as the mortifying gurgle continued.

The tension broke and she giggled too.

'You haven't eaten all day,' he said reprovingly. 'You barely left your desk.'

He'd noticed that? And now he intercepted the amazed look she shot him and countered it with a smile.

'Of course not, you might've locked me out if I left the building,' she answered. 'And you were in your office all day too.' She struggled not to react too obviously to his distracting charm—how could he have gone from infuriating to fascinating like this?

'You were watching me?' His eyebrow quirked.

'I was prudently keeping an eye on a *threat*, yes.'

'A threat?' he teased with mock outrage. 'Little old me?'

Oh, the man totally knew the impact he had on people—most especially women.

'You were all for throwing me out of the building,' she said. 'And I need my job.'

'You've saved your job.' His expression turned serious again. 'But I had my lunch delivered, whereas *you* need food *now*.'

'And I'll get it. *Shortly*.' Though she had no idea if Juno had any in her apartment. Or whether there was a store nearby. Not that she had any cash to buy anything with.

'Push that button.'

'Pardon?'

Alvaro leaned across, reaching past her to touch a discreet button. The glove compartment slid open with controlled smoothness and a light automatically illuminated the interior.

'Oh. Wow.' She stared at the incredibly ordered contents in the surprisingly large space.

'Help yourself,' he invited.

'You get hungry?'

'What kind of a question is that to ask a man my height?'

She resisted the urge to feast her eyes on his physique yet again. She was already far too aware of his height and muscularity and doubtless he did need a tonne of food to keep his...*energy* up. And she needed an immediate distraction from her shockingly inappropriate thoughts.

'What's this one?' She pulled out one bright rectangular package.

'Protein bar. They're pretty much all protein bars.'

'Do you carry them on you too?'

'Sure. I go too long without fuel, I get ugly.'

Laughter bubbled out of her before she could stop it. The concepts of 'Alvaro' and 'ugly' were absolute opposites of the reality spectrum. 'So, an endless supply of protein bars?'

'And fruit bars, sometimes chocolate bars...' He shrugged.

'This isn't just a bar at the bottom of your bag.' She gazed at the compartment again. There had to be at least twenty different bars in there. 'This is like survivalist mode.'

'Like I'm prepped for the zombie apocalypse?' He reached past her again and picked one with a scarlet and black wrapper, expertly tearing it and taking a bite while still driving.

'You ever gone hungry for days on end?' he asked after a moment.

'No.' She'd never gone without. Her meals had always been perfectly nutritionally balanced affairs, carefully prepared by the palace chefs. They still were. And she still put up with the annoying monthly medical checks with the palace physician—as she had all her life—because her advisors expected it. It was, now she thought about it, ridiculously over the top.

'It's not a nice feeling,' he said.

She gazed at him, but he didn't add anything more, he was too busy chewing. Deliberately avoiding answering her unspoken questions, she realised. A horrible sensation washed through her. Alvaro knew that feeling of hunger *well*. And she'd just been mentally moaning about her privileged palace food.

'Go on, try it,' he encouraged after a while, nodding to the bar she still held. 'Don't be polite, I know you're starving.'

For diversion from those horrible thoughts as much as anything, she unwrapped it and took a bite.

'Well?' he asked, that laugh back in his voice.

'It's actually...not bad.' She nodded.

'I know.' He laughed. 'Take another for later.'

'I can't do that.'

'Why not? As you can see, I have plenty.'

'Do you get through them or do they get old and go to waste?'

'None go to waste.'

She heard that hint of history again in the serious edge of his answer.

'I give them away if they start to get too old. I don't throw food out.' Alvaro shook his head, regretting the small truths escaping him the way air escaped through the smallest tear in a once-tight seal.

He never discussed personal things, never answered to anyone, never hinted at what had once been… His past was irrelevant; his reasons for his action remained his own.

Yet here he was, telling her little truths that added up to a horror story. She wouldn't know that though. She'd think he was just a perpetually hungry man mountain.

He tried to clear his head, but the scent of vanilla permeated the air. It wasn't from the stupid snacks, it was her. He'd noticed it before and now, in the close confines of the car, it tantalised—making his mouth water and his body tense. He liked vanilla, a lot.

She'd fallen silent again, apparently focused on the road he was taking. Ironically *her* reticence bothered him more than the lapse of his own. She'd smiled at him before with that same open smile he'd seen first thing this morning when, oblivious to his presence, she'd got to her desk. When she'd turned it on him, it had almost caused him to veer off the road. But now she'd stilled, masking those turbulent emotions. He itched to brush the veil from her eyes so that mobility of expression was revealed. Because it was there. She was more sensitive, more volatile than he'd expected and yet, most of the time, so *controlled*.

He couldn't shake the suspicion she was somehow vulnerable—which was stupid when she could clearly take care of herself. She didn't need him getting all unnecessarily gallant… But he couldn't stop his acute awareness of her, while a million and more questions mushroomed in his mind. Because while he couldn't put his finger on it, something was off. Maybe the feeling was merely a residual hangover from that social media mess.

He should've cut himself free of that old app a while ago, but it had been his first success and he'd been loath to lose anything from his arsenal of enterprise. Back when Plan A—to be a professional sportsman—had been destroyed when the ligaments in his knee had been torn, that little idea he'd had, when he'd been captain of the school basketball, football and volleyball teams all at once, had come into its own. He'd been desperate not just to survive, but to succeed at getting out of the poverty hell he'd been in for ever. To escape that insecurity and lift his elderly foster carer, Ellen, with him. And he had. All on his own—with the determined independence he still treasured.

'This is where you live?' he asked.

It was his navigation system, not Juno, who confirmed it. And his discomfort grew. The rundown building on the edge of Queens looked as if it needed a better landlord. It was hardly a palace for a princess. Alvaro pulled over in front of it, his muscles clenching as he glanced around the darkened neighbourhood.

'Thank you for the lift. I so appreciate it,' she said with slightly haughty dismissiveness.

But he was already out of the car. It was too late and the corners too dark for him to leave her yet. He used to meet Ellen and they'd walk home together from night shifts. He'd never leave anyone to walk streets like this alone. He picked up Juno's case, followed her up the stairs and waited while she fished in her purse for the key.

'What's wrong?' he asked eventually.

'Nothing.'

The raw edge in her answer set his nerves on edge. Something was wrong. He leaned past and saw her struggling with the door. 'Can I help?'

'I just...' She looked mortified. 'It sticks sometimes.'

So, the last thing she wanted right now was to accept more help from him? Frankly, that put him out. 'Let me have a go.'

Silently she held out the key.

'You don't have any security guard or anything?' He glanced down the side alleyway, loathing the still shadows and the thought of her arriving here alone night after night.

'No,' she murmured.

'But you're a bona fide princess.'

'Not really.' She sounded choked. 'They changed the line of succession after my mother and I left.'

'And cast you out into the world, alone and defenceless?' he muttered as he forced the key to turn in the half-rusted lock. He didn't know too much about the situation in her home country, but it didn't sound right.

She stiffened beside him and he heard her sharply inhale.

'I can take care of myself,' she said valiantly.

Jade cringed as she stepped over the threshold. It was *such* a lie. How could she claim that when she didn't even know which of these doors off the vestibule led to Juno's apartment?

Panic rose. She couldn't pull this off. She didn't have any cash, didn't know where to get food or how to even order a damn pizza. Now she had to go into the office for another few days and pretend she was the capable, smart and savvy Juno. It was mortifying.

She'd never made a meal in her life. Everything had been brought to her. She was the *definition* of spoilt—to be so incompetent in all basic life skills? She'd been supposed to come here and eat pizza and doughnuts without being judged, to walk around sightseeing, blending in like any other tourist, childishly soaking up the Christmas lights and candy... It was supposed to be her secret escape, a few days of anonymous freedom. Only now?

Alvaro's mouth compressed as he gazed down at her as she stood frozen in the open doorway.

'It's not right to deny someone their birthright.

To take away their identity and place in the world,' he said roughly.

Once again, his tone held an emotional, personal edge she didn't understand and hadn't expected. What did he know of identity and loss? Obviously something, because he was right.

'I know,' she said huskily.

She burned with guilt at lying to him, yet his empathy drew her to him at the same time. She had the most appalling urge to lean close—not for the safety or the security a big strong man like him could offer. But for quite the opposite— something far more tempting, far more dangerous.

She didn't, of course. She stiffened and forced herself to step further into the relative safety of the building. She was *not* screwing this up for Juno. But she wished her twin had told her how ridiculously attractive Alvaro was, because her inability to cope with the reality of him was something terrible. If only she'd known.

'Goodnight, Juno.'

For once in her life Jade couldn't execute a polite reply. She simply nodded and closed the door, before leaning against it to stop herself opening it again and saying something stupid.

Why now? Why *him*?

She'd met several attractive men: advisors, guests, even King Leonardo of Severene—who her father and his advisors suggested would be a suitable husband…

But she'd never felt her pulse skip and sprint the way it did around Alvaro. She'd never felt restless or had an ache burning deep and low in those secret parts that had stayed resolutely silent before.

How was she to survive the next few days with Alvaro Byrne as her boss?

It was impossible.

CHAPTER FOUR

'So, Juno—'

'Please,' Jade interrupted Grace, another of the social media assistants. 'Please call me PJ.'

'PJ?' Alvaro, sitting just along from her, frowned.

'Yes.' She forced a smile and grabbed assertiveness with both hands. 'For—'

'Pineapple Juice?' Grace joked.

'Plain Jane?' Jade giggled back.

'Poor Joke?' Alvaro added blandly.

Jade shot him a look. 'Yes, it's a new thing, but it's good to refresh, right?'

'Refresh?' Alvaro echoed.

'Like we need to do with some of your social media channels,' she said with more bravery than she felt. As a comeback it was weak, but it was the best she could muster in front of everyone.

It was her own fault that he was watching her with that wary, almost disapproving eye. She'd been late, thanks to figuring out the damn subway system again, which would've been fine except he was waiting by her desk to ask her to join in this never-ending meeting with so many other people.

'You did an amazing job turning this issue around for us yesterday,' Sophy, the marketing manager, filled the sharp little silence. 'It's the honesty and authenticity that people have responded to.'

Jade wasn't either honest or authentic. She was sitting here lying to them all right this second. And she couldn't bear to look at the tall man sitting to her left, yet she couldn't seem to stop herself. Her pulse still wouldn't settle but worse was the heightened state of awareness, the heat, the craving she felt for his attention.

'Are you all okay to work through lunch?' Alvaro asked. 'I've ordered catering.'

A noisy cheer echoed around the meeting room. Jade's stomach cheered too. Turned out Juno didn't keep her fridge well stocked and Jade hadn't had time to stop to get anything on the way to work this morning. So yes, she was starving again.

'Lunch is important, after all. To keep us going.' Alvaro's gaze landed on Jade again. 'And it's our last week before our Christmas break, right?'

Try as hard as she could, she couldn't tear her gaze from that knowing glint in his—as if he'd somehow twigged she'd gone without again and he'd deliberately ordered in.

'And the sooner we refine these plans, the sooner we can break up early,' he added.

While the rest of the staff looked delighted, Jade wished she could melt and slide into a gooey mess under the meeting table. She *never* tripped over her words. She never felt *nerves* like this. But she was far too conscious of him.

'Can you work up a proposal, PJ?' Sophy asked. 'It doesn't have to be fully costed or detailed. I'd just like the concept to mull over during the Christmas break.'

'Of course.' Jade scrambled to catch up on what it was they'd been saying and on what topic it was she was supposed to propose…and she'd get to researching 'how to write a proposal' the second she was back at her desk.

'Wow, did you get hair extensions?' Grace paused beside her when they finally stood to leave the meeting room, almost three hours later.

'Pardon?' Jade lifted her hand to her head and realised some of her hair had fallen from the top-knot she'd tied it in early this morning, and it was now hanging in a long streak over her shoulder. 'Oh, yes, I did.'

'It looks amazing. I love the length and the colour.'

'Thank you.'

But yet again her errant, apparently uncontrollable gaze glided across the room to collide with Alvaro Byrne's once more. He impacted every sense—her vision and hearing were so attuned to him, but most of all he struck a need for touch within her. It was appallingly inappropriate. Even after the meeting—after he was locked away in his own office—he still oozed animal magnetism, dominating every damn one of her thoughts. It was as if she'd walked into a cloud of heated, sensual fog. She couldn't see beyond him, couldn't think of anything else. It was *mortifying*—mostly because it seemed so beyond her control.

There were plenty of other men in the office and there were those personal trainer guys who worked at the gym downstairs who walked around with equally ripped muscles on show all the time... But none of them had the effect on her that Alvaro Byrne did, even now when he was covered up in his perfectly tailored suit.

The worst thing, though, was that she was sure *he* was aware of her response to him. There was an arrogant tilt to his lips and an astute glint in his heavy gaze, as if he could see through her superficial layer to that guilt just beneath. He watched her as if he knew, or at least suspected, something was wrong.

And he was right, of course.

She didn't want to wreck Juno's reputation, but she didn't think she could sustain this lie. She'd gone too public and what had been a minor error was now getting more attention than before. That online bulletin had asked again to interview *her*— it was ridiculous—and more people were trying to follow her online. Thank goodness Juno had shut down her social media platforms because, as it was, some of her old pictures had been recirculating. If anyone looked too closely and spotted any differences between them and the 'Juno' in the office now? It was a nightmare waiting to come to life.

But it was that internal battle that was the most hideous. She'd prided herself on her ability to contain her emotions, to be the calm, polite princess who could control her own thoughts and get the job done. But all that control had slid the second she'd encountered Alvaro Byrne.

And now she'd got to know a little of him? He wasn't the autocratic bully who didn't bother to listen…in reality he did hear, he did see. He even apologised.

Which meant he was impossible to stay mad with, impossible to say no to, impossible to ignore. But he was her boss. So she had to. Because he was so, *so* out of bounds.

Something still didn't add up. And that fact that he was still obsessing over her *days* later? Alvaro couldn't wait for tomorrow—Friday, finally. The office was officially closing for Christmas and it would give him a few days alone to sort out his head—and other parts. Because he did *not* screw around with employees. Ever. It wasn't as if he hadn't had the chance. He'd had to be very distanced from one former recruit who'd made a pass at him, but he didn't like it messy in the workplace.

Outside the company? For a while seduction had been a sport like any other, and Alvaro always played to win. But he'd matured since the days when he'd taken what had been offered just because he could. And he'd swiftly learned it was simpler to stay single. With his workload he couldn't meet the commitment or expectations of a long-term relationship. Nowadays he enjoyed an occasional brief affair with a woman willing to enjoy the lifestyle—and lack of strings—he offered. A woman unencumbered by unrealistic dreams of happy-ever-after, or drama.

But this woman? An employee. A princess— even if cast off from her kingdom… There was so much drama. So much that was forbidden.

Yet he couldn't tear his attention from her. Couldn't stop the urges whispering within— they'd been his constant, irritating companions every minute since he'd sparred with her first thing last Monday morning. Every day since had only added to the weight of temptation. And his curiosity—sexual and otherwise—had equally magnified as the days had passed.

Why had a supposedly streetwise 'rebel' struggled to unlock her own front door? Why had she fleetingly looked panicked when she had been late the other day? And he couldn't be sure, but he suspected that for some reason she wasn't eating

much. He'd seen her pour herself too many coffees from the office filter, adding doses of sugar
and cream as if to magically bulk it into a meal...
He was probably projecting his own old feelings
and fear of hunger on that one, but he'd ordered
lunch into the meeting on Tuesday just in case.
He'd done the same again every day since, calling
it his new Christmas tradition. As if he knew anything about those. But he couldn't stand to think of
someone starving. Sometimes she seemed miles
away—Sophy had had to call her name twice the
other day. And her immediate apology, the polite
smile she offered? The stillness in the way she sat?
Her quietness in the office? She was a contradiction. Because he knew that, beneath that supposedly serene exterior, she was stifling a snappy
fighter. He wanted *that* Juno to emerge again. Instead, she'd buried herself in that stupid proposal
Sophy had requested.

He'd had to resist, employing every ounce of
self-control not to try and provoke the feisty determination he'd discovered lay beneath that poised
facade. She was *too* perfectly contained. Where
was the wild 'Rebel Princess' her old social media
posts showed her to be? Where was the flash of
spirit she'd shown him on Monday morning?

While she looked the same, she didn't *seem*
the same.

But *he* didn't need to be wasting his time contemplating her. It was the slide into the holiday

season, right? Maybe he'd fixated on her as a distraction from all the happy family, festive tinsel stuff filling the city. Speaking of which, he clicked into his email system to check that his orders to Ellen had been delivered. His foster carer had always worked Christmas, as had he as soon as he was able. He still did. Satisfied when he saw the receipts were signed off, he pushed back from his desk and stood. Thankfully it was Thursday night and he'd made it. He'd not gone near her, not noticed those slim-fitting black trousers and pristine white shirt. He'd ignored the fact that his fingers itched to skim over her lines and that he ached to discover what softness and curves lay beneath…

His staff were going out tonight, celebrating the holiday starting tomorrow. He'd never been more glad that he'd agreed to close the office a few days ahead of Christmas. He told his assistant to pass on his good wishes. They were used to him not stopping in to socialise.

He took the stairs down to the gym, once more trying to work out the never-ending frustration, knowing that when he got back, she would be gone and out of reach. The relief would be immense. Avoidance was his only remaining strategy.

But when he returned to the office in gym shorts and tee, a full fifty minutes later, she was still sitting at her desk, still in that same self-contained pose, still silently focused on her screen. The only other person on the floor.

'*What* are you doing?' he demanded, his patience blown.

'Oh!' She spun on her chair and drew in a shocked breath. Her jade eyes widened.

Déjà-vu. Suddenly he was hotter than he'd been mid-workout. Because once again she was staring at him as if she'd never seen a man before. Honestly, it took everything not to flex. But every muscle was already tense—they'd been on high alert for days.

'I thought you worked out this morning,' she blurted, then blushed.

Alvaro smiled faintly. She taken note of his routine? Good, because he'd been barely able to tear his attention from her for days now.

'I did,' he said. 'I work out twice a day. It's how I manage stress.'

It was a discipline too. The habit branded within him from his youth. He'd learned that if he wanted to succeed at something, he had to work harder, longer, heavier, than any competitor. Only this time his competitor was his own lust. So in fact he'd gone for another session in the middle of the day today, desperate to burn some of the energy coiling tighter and tighter within him.

'I'm sorry you're stressed.' She bit her lip. 'I don't think I've helped you there.'

That was incredibly true, but not in the way she meant.

'It's habit as well.' He shrugged, trying to rein

himself in and at least act casual. 'Twice a day, every day. I like it.'

Another blush swept across her cheeks. He stared. Was she interested in what he *liked*? In what made him feel *good*? Because really, the best thing of all was the most instinctive, the most animal of urges…was she thinking about sex? Because he not so suddenly was. Damn, if he didn't have the overriding instinct that the chemistry between them would be instantly combustible.

'Why are you still here?' He growled, irritated with his one-track mind. 'The others have gone for Christmas drinks.'

'I know.' Her expression pinched. 'But I wanted to finish up that report before leaving.'

'There's always tomorrow morning.'

'I don't want to leave it until the last minute. I want to be sure it's done and done well.'

Seriously perfect, wasn't she? His skin seemed to have shrunk too small for his muscles. Why didn't the 'Rebel Princess' want to party? He'd overheard one of the guys ask her out yesterday and she'd made some weak excuse about getting home to her cat. But there'd been a large 'no pets' sign at the entrance of her apartment building the other day and definitely no felines yowling around. She'd been lying.

'You're not going to join them?' Her glance was wary as he silently stared at her.

'I'm the boss. They'll have more fun if I'm not casting a shadow over proceedings.'

Jade stood, her nerves too strained for her to remain still. He was no shadow. He was a light that commanded all attention, who made her incredibly aware of every movement, every breath. She needed to *leave*.

She couldn't believe she'd come across him in his wretched workout gear all over again. This time he hadn't stripped, he still had a tee shirt on. But the arms on show? The skin? All those muscles? It was impossible not to stare even as she burned to a crisp, her brain overcooked and immediately unproductive. She'd been struggling all week—hyper-aware, absurdly impressed. And it was evident his staff were completely loyal—no wonder they'd all phoned Juno so desperately when that little post had gone awry. They would do anything for him and no wonder—with his patience in meetings, his insights, and those incredible catered lunches?

Yes. She had to get out of there. *Now.* Before she did something mortifying. Because now he was nearer, now there was an element in those amber eyes that expressed…*care.*

'Are you okay?' His voice was low and husky and soothing. 'Juno?'

She closed her eyes. She hated hearing her sister's name on his lips. She hated that she'd lied to anyone, but most of all him. And she hated how much his opinion of her mattered to her.

'I'm not used to…' *Having a stunning man stand so close.* She opened her eyes and sighed. 'I'm just a bit tired.'

'You've had a tough week.' He was looking at her as if he were trying to solve a puzzle. 'What do you do to unwind? If it's not heading out for a drink and it's not burning off stress in a gym…'

She froze. The only other thing she could think of was the one thing she'd *never* done with anyone. Why was that utterly inappropriate suggestion leaping into her mind now and flashing like an unavoidable neon sign?

'What are you going to do?' A frown intensified the amber depth of his warm eyes. 'You're obviously strung out.'

She'd thought she'd done a good job of holding herself together, and he was telling her everyone could see right through her?

'You're pale. When did you last eat?'

'Actually, I had a protein bar for afternoon tea.' And that was after a huge sandwich from that lunch he'd had delivered.

His mouth quirked but he shook his head slightly. 'Not enough.'

'A protein bar lasts a long time.'

'Rot.'

'Maybe my engine doesn't need the same amount of fuel as yours.'

His gaze drilled into hers. 'All engines need good fuel and good, regular service.'

She suppressed a shiver. She was misinterpreting what he was saying, reading something inappropriate into every word.

She tried to laugh. 'You take this interest in all your staff?'

She felt his tension immediately treble.

'You've had a difficult few days,' he clipped. 'Dealing with that stuff online can become overwhelming, even when mistakes haven't been made. I want to make sure you're okay.'

'I'm okay.' She forced a smile. 'Thank you.'

'Are you sure?'

This didn't feel like a normal conversation between boss and employee, or colleagues, or even friends. This was heavier. Her heart thudded, bolting her in place right there before him. He didn't move either. The world telescoped. They were inches apart and no one else was there and there was no threat of interruption…and the longing sweeping through her was crazy. Any rational capacity lapsed, leaving only the ache of temptation. Her limbs trembled as yearning flooded. It was almost a dream when he slowly lifted his hand and lifted a lock of her hair, then ran it through his fingers. She held her breath, not wanting to move, not wanting this mirage to end.

'It's so long,' he muttered. 'I can't believe it isn't real.'

She sucked in a breath as hurt whistled through her. He'd heard her lie and lie and lie and every one burned. She *never* should have thought this switch was a good idea. Yet, if she hadn't, she never would have met Alvaro. She would never have had this moment. Suddenly the urge to lean into his light touch was unstoppable. 'I...'

He blinked and jerked his hand away in a negating gesture and she knew he was about to step back. But she didn't want anything to spoil this one, precious moment. She couldn't.

'It is real,' she blurted, so lost in staring up at him that she lost control of her tongue, telling him things she shouldn't. But she'd never been drawn to anyone the way she was to him. She needed him to *see* her—truly.

'What?' He stood like a hot granite statue.

'My hair,' she muttered helplessly, so stupidly. 'It's real. It's mine.'

His eyebrows pleated. 'But—'

'I'm not Juno.'

His mouth opened.

'I'm...' She paused to swallow, horrified yet unable to halt her confession. She didn't even want to. She wanted—needed—him to know the truth. 'I'm not Juno Monroyale.'

'What?' While his eyes widened, their focus was laser-like.

'I'm her sister.'

For an endless moment neither moved. But beyond his unnatural stillness she knew he was processing and she could feel his reaction rising. A howling heat emanated from his tense body, while loss welled in hers. She'd broken his trust, so now she braced for his fury.

But what emerged was almost a whisper. 'You're not Juno.' He stared so hard he paralysed her. 'If you're not Juno…'

She was Jade. She was the Queen of Monrova.

Confessions were supposed to relieve, instead desolation slid deep, painfully making hidden cuts, as she watched him make the connection.

'Then that means…' He trailed off again, his focus still intent upon her. But as he blinked, the reaction behind his frozen countenance flared and she saw a blaze of emotion heating his whisky-amber eyes.

'If you're not Juno,' he said harshly, 'then I'm not your boss.'

He suddenly stepped forward and that desolation was swept away by a tsunami of something so much hotter. So much more that she couldn't think to answer.

'I'm not your boss,' he repeated angrily, almost to himself.

And she realised that he'd just let something within himself go.

His hand hit her waist in a firm, heavy hold that made her heart thud. She couldn't tear her gaze from his—couldn't move, or speak. Her lips parted, yet she still couldn't breathe as an enormous wave of want tumbled over her again, drenching her with a desire so powerful it knocked over any hesitation, any caution, any reality. All she could hear was her heated blood beating, all she wanted was the touch she'd craved for days.

Just a taste.

She still couldn't speak as he pulled her so close her breasts were pressed against the sizzling strength of his chest, nor could she speak as he slid his other hand to cup the nape of her neck. And she still couldn't say a thing as she leaned against his hold, arching her neck to maintain that impossibly intense contact with his gaze. And then, beneath that penetrating stare, she realised she didn't need to speak. Nor did he. They both knew the answer was obvious and undeniable. In reality, there wasn't even a question.

His head lowered and her breath released on a gasp just as his mouth slammed on hers, his strength making her knees buckle. His hold instantly tightened, and he hauled her fully against him. The impact of collision—chest to breast, hip to hip—destroyed her. His heat, his arousal, made hers burn hotter. She was literally caught up in his passion and his vitality and she could do nothing but be carried along the road he'd chosen. The sensuality poured from him, filling and stirring her, until she had no choice but to release her own, kissing him back as best she could beneath his onslaught, clutching his shoulders, not just to touch, but to hold—to *keep*. Because she needed more of this. Of *him*. She needed so much more. She burst with the need to race with him, to beat him, to hit some near-but-far dizzying destination. Oh, she was suddenly so, so desperate.

Somehow he spun them both and moved her back until the wall was behind her. It was literally the hard place supporting her while he— like a rock in front—crushed closer, caressing her, kissing her sensitive lips with unrestrained passion. And it was so good because he was so big, so powerful and every muscle, every movement was utterly focused on her. Initially she'd been stunned, rendered immobile, but with each sweep of his plundering tongue her response rose, drawn out of her like a release of a power she'd not known she had. And then she didn't just open for him, she met him with a seeking, demanding slice of her own force. Every particle within her tensed and tingled, filled with energy that couldn't be contained.

These weren't soft, gentle, teasing kisses. These devoured. Fast and long and hot as pent-up passion exploded. It was an almost animalistic seeking to sate long aching hunger. He kissed her as if he'd been thinking of nothing else for eons and she kissed him back just like that because for her it was true. She tightened her arms around his neck, threading her fingers through his unruly thick hair and holding him to her. His fingers slid beneath her shirt, caressing her waist, lifting higher to smooth her ribcage, and she leaned into the sweep of his palm, all her skin ablaze, aching for such touch from him over every inch—inside and out. Exhilaration soared. Her toes curled and she pressed her hips forward, grinding them back against his to feel the shockingly huge reality of his arousal. Heated pleasure stormed, setting off a volley of vibrations within. Lust coiled higher still, the yearning inside widened. His hand at her breast. The scrape of his thumb across her nipple. The ache to be naked. All consumed her.

'Alvaro...'

He smothered hot, wide kisses across her face and down her neck and his hips pressed against hers again and again, mimicking the ultimate act of passion and possession. Never had she felt such excitement, such abandonment. Never had she wanted anything as much. Never had anything so instinctive overtaken her so completely. She cried out as he savagely sucked, then nipped, her sensitive skin.

'J—' He broke off the guttural mutter and abruptly flung back from her, leaving her slumped back against the wall.

Shocked and suddenly cold, she put her hands palm down for balance, absorbing certainty from the solid wall as she watched him transform before her in the blink of an eye—from passionate lover to furious stranger.

His hair stood in tufts from where she'd tugged at him like some untamed creature. His chest rapidly rose and fell and there was a wild look in his eyes. But his glare solidified and scoured her insides. 'If you're not Juno, then you're...'

Her lips felt puffy and oversensitive and she couldn't bear to press them together. She licked them but it didn't soothe their hungry ache. And she had to answer him. 'Jade.'

His hands curled in fists and he jammed them onto his hips, his chest rising and falling as if he'd just run a life-or-death sprint. 'Juno's identical twin sister.'

'Yes,' she confessed. But his angry reaction horrified her. 'I'm sorry you thought I was her.' Oh, God, she realised the worst and whispered, 'You wanted to kiss her.'

'What? *No!*' His frown deepened. 'I've never wanted to kiss Juno. Never wanted to order her into my office and slam the door behind her so I could grab her and strip her—' He broke off and cursed—a full sentence of self-berating filth.

She stared at him as something feral inside roared with primal pleasure. Every millimetre of her skin tightened again with awareness and want.

'I've never wanted to do that with *any* of my employees,' he said more calmly a few moments later. 'I've never been unable to control my reaction to anyone before.'

'But your reaction to me?' Her mouth dried because she was stupidly nervous. As if she were facing all the exams of her life in the one moment. Pass or fail were the only options. Win or lose. Have or have not. She wanted to win. She wanted to have.

Just this one moment.

But she could see him calculating and she could feel him cooling...so quickly. His emotional withdrawal wasn't just visible, wasn't just audible, it was palpable. And she felt it as the devastating loss it was. She wanted his heat, his body, his intimacy. For once in her life, she wanted to obliterate her isolation.

'If you're Jade,' he said quietly, 'you're the Queen.'

Her heart dropped to the floor, but she tried to pull herself together, to answer with her old, customary politeness. 'That's correct.'

The change in the atmosphere was as strong as if a foehn wind had lifted and turned all the fallen leaves over, presenting the whole world in a different colour.

But it wasn't the whole world. It was only her. *She* was being seen in a new light. No longer an employee. No longer a woman.

She was merely—*only*—a monarch.

CHAPTER FIVE

'YOU SWITCHED PLACES,' Alvaro said with cold clarity. 'At the weekend.'

'Yes,' Jade admitted miserably, mortified by her unthinkable, inappropriate actions. All of them. 'I'm...'

Unable to think.

Why had she said anything at all? Why had she betrayed Juno so swiftly? She'd only been here a few days and she'd let desire overrule everything. She'd *never* let personal wishes get in the way of professional duty before. And her duty right now was to Juno. She'd let her sister down badly. But she'd not been able to resist him any longer, and certainly not been able to lie to him any longer.

'What are you playing at?' He watched her from those few paces back. *'Why?'*

'Juno needed time in Monrova.' But without further explanation her reason sounded weak. Yet those reasons were private to Juno.

His fists tightened. 'You lied. Not just to me, but to everyone.'

'To protect my sister, yes. I'm sorry. It wasn't just for fun. It *mattered* more than that.'

'Not just for your sister. You wouldn't take such a big risk if there wasn't something in it for you too. Something that *matters*.' He echoed her emphasis, but his had an edge. 'So what is it?'

'It's just a few weeks,' she muttered, glad of the steadying wall supporting her back. 'But it's the only chance I was ever going to get to be…a normal person.'

'Normal?'

'As normal as either Juno and I can get.' And yes, she knew she sounded like the ultimate spoilt princess right now.

But he nodded, as if understanding. 'A few weeks—in a lifetime?'

'Yes.'

'Yet you're spending them working round the clock on some stupid job for me?'

'For my *sister*. I don't want her to lose this—'

'She won't.'

'Thank you.' She couldn't bear to look at him.

'Does she know what's happened here at work?'

'We've not been in touch since we switched. We thought it was safer not to.'

'Safer?' He sounded astounded. 'It's a shocking risk you've taken. I *knew* something was off.' He expelled a harsh breath. 'Why have you told me now?'

'Why do you think?' she mumbled. 'I...was drawn to you.'

Such an understatement. The real risk was what she'd just done and the terrible thing was she wanted more. The sheer rush still rampaging through her.

'Nothing more can happen between us, Jade. You're a *queen*.'

His immediate rejection hurt. 'Am I suddenly inhuman?'

'Aren't you supposed to be engaged to another man?' he threw back at her. 'Don't you have to marry some prince?'

Shocked, she stared at him. Had he heard the rumours about King Leonardo of Severene? It was what her father had wanted and the plan had still been progressing. She'd been supposed to give King Leonardo an indication of her willingness at the Winter Ball. Instead she'd run away—seizing on Juno's mad switch suggestion to stop herself having to make that decision just yet. She'd literally run away from it.

Ironically now Jade seized that exact prospect as a way of putting a barrier between her newfound recklessness and her duty. Because of her own weakness, she needed to put Alvaro at a distance. *Now.*

Yet she couldn't lie to him completely. 'Nothing has been settled.'

His eyebrows shot up. 'But it's under consideration?'

'Several options are…' She fudged, but he silently waited her out. 'It's more like a…political contract. An alliance to benefit both our countries.'

'You'd really marry for duty?'

'If that's what's required,' she said determinedly. 'It wouldn't be the first time it's happened in history.'

He stepped closer and her wretched body hummed with temptation anew.

'What's in the fine print?' His voice was both harsh and husky, that thread of anger strengthened. 'Would you produce heirs?'

'Of course,' she said stiffly. 'For the succession. We would have a shared heir between Severene and Monrova.'

'And unite the two into one country? So this is an acquisition? Who'll have the greater power— Monrova or Severene?'

Jade straightened. She would never cede power over Monrova to another nation. Not even a friendly neighbour like Severene. It would be an *alliance*. But Alvaro's distaste grew more evident with every sarcastically enunciated question.

'Does this prince of yours expect you to be a virgin queen?' he asked. 'Is that part of your promise too?'

'I imagine he'd think my virginity is a hindrance, actually,' Jade retorted, stung by Alvaro's judgment. 'He probably wouldn't be at all pleased.'

'You...*what?*' Alvaro's eyes widened. 'He *what?*'

She realised he'd not expected her to answer that virginity question—let alone honestly.

'Well, it is inconvenient,' she said, explaining it with bald businesslike briskness to cover her embarrassment. 'But neither of us would consider sex as anything other than a biological transaction. Fortunately, there are other ways for me to become pregnant.'

'What?' He actually gasped. 'Are you talking about artificial insemination?'

She shrugged. 'It might be a preferable option for us both.'

His jaw slack, he slowly shook his head. 'You're a virgin. An actual, real-life twenty-something virgin.'

'I'm sure I'm not the only one in existence,' she retorted testily. 'But I've been very sheltered all my life.' All but imprisoned, to be more accurate. 'There really hasn't been the opportunity.'

He stared at her, then glanced away, visibly processing it all. A few moments passed and she felt relieved that the subject was closed. But then he faced her again—muscles flexing as he moved, the faint sheen of sweat making his bronzed skin glow.

'Have you ever kissed anyone else?' It was a whisper.

One she couldn't answer.

'Jade?' Alarm flashed across his face, but he stepped closer again.

She was indescribably pleased by that small shrinking of that gap between them, but there was no hiding the obvious truth.

'Never?' He lifted his hand and brushed her lip with his fingertip. 'I'm sorry. Did I hurt you?'

'No,' she breathed. And she didn't want him to be sorry.

'It was a little more than a kiss.' His frown hadn't fully eased, but there was the smallest quirk of his lips as he softly questioned her. 'What did you think?'

That blush burned again. 'You know already...'

He waited but she couldn't say more.

'Are you always this careful with your words? This...reticent?' That quirk became a complete smile. 'Not officially a risk taker, Queen Jade?' He leaned closer. 'Yet I think you're *exactly* that.' He brushed her lower lip with that lightest of fingertips again. 'Is that the real reason you switched with Juno? So you could have a couple of weeks to sow all the wild oats you can?'

That smile, that touch, provoked her. 'Would it be so awful if it was?' she challenged, even though it had been nothing of the sort. 'Why shouldn't I? King Leonardo has certainly enjoyed life to the full. There shouldn't be a reason why I can't do the same.'

Alvaro's frown instantly returned. 'Are you really considering marriage to him?'

She paused.

'You don't see something wrong with fooling around with me here while considering that?'

She stiffened. 'The moment I make any marriage vows, I intend to keep them.'

'But haven't you made a promise already? Isn't that what an engagement is?'

'I'm not engaged to *anyone*,' she declared hotly. 'I'll do that at the time required. Until then, *everything* is my own.'

He suddenly leaned his shoulder against the wall next to her, facing her, *watching* her. 'You're using semantics. You're twisting it to get what you want.'

'Well, why shouldn't I get what I want for once?' She lifted her chin. 'I'm prepared to do everything for my country. I'll sacrifice my personal life to perform my duty.' She threw her shoulders back. 'But I've not yet made that promise to King Leonardo. Not him or any other man.'

'Would it be a very convenient marriage—with you both having affairs on the side?'

'I can't speak for anyone else. But if *I* ever marry, I have every intention of maintaining my vows.'

'You'd settle for a sexless life?'

She was burning with mortification at his relentless questioning. 'I've gone without sex up until now—I'm confident I can go without it for decades.'

But something went cold inside. Only now did she realise the gravity of her future choices.

'Wow. You're quite the willing martyr.' His eyes flashed. 'But you won't expect that from your husband?'

'I'd expect him to live with his own decisions, as we all must. And I don't intend to hold any of his decisions against him. I understand the sacrifice we must both make.'

'That's the biggest load of horse shit I've ever heard in my life.' Alvaro straightened, only to step closer still. 'So you're going to calmly turn a blind eye to all his affairs? You're going to let him parade his lovers in front of you?'

'Leonardo is not a monster. He cares about his kingdom and if he wanted to…to…' She trailed off, hating to even think of Leonardo in any kind of sexual way. He was like distant family to her. 'I'm sure he'd be discreet. We both want what's best for both our countries. We would come to an understanding.'

'Some understanding,' Alvaro scoffed. 'He gets to do what he wants while you get to die of boredom.'

She glared at him. 'I don't think that sex is the be-all and end-all of a fulfilling life.'

Alvaro laughed and she lost it.

'Look, if I desperately want an orgasm,' she snapped, 'I can give myself one.'

His jaw dropped. 'Sure,' he almost wheezed. 'Of course, you can and should…frequently, I would hope.'

She was mortified that she'd stumbled into this subject so blindly.

'But…' He cocked his head. 'You know how they say a trouble shared is a trouble halved?'

She nodded, mildly confused.

'They also say a pleasure shared is a pleasure doubled.'

'No one says that.'

'Maybe not, but that doesn't mean it isn't true.' He took a length of her hair, looped it around his fingers and leaned closer still. 'And you don't know that yet, do you?'

It was a whisper of a kiss, a brush so light and tempting that all caution slid from her again. And then there was another kiss—all temptation, all gentle, sweet tease. He was so hot. But beneath that tender touch, there was the promise of fire— that unleashed passion he'd swept her into only minutes before. She wanted both kinds—*now*. And when he lifted his mouth a millimetre from hers, she couldn't stay silent.

'Show me, then,' she breathed.

'So that's what you want, Queen Jade?'

'You? Yes.' She swallowed, but now her desire outweighed her embarrassment again. 'I don't

know why it is. Part of me wishes it wasn't you…
there's that cute guy who delivers the post—'

'Vito?' Alvaro lifted his head and barked. '*Not*
for you.'

She exploded too—in pure frustration. 'I'm attracted to you. I like kissing you. And I want to
explore—' She hauled back her self-control, trying to explain herself. 'But I understand if, given
everything you've just learned, that's not what
you want.'

'You understand?' Alvaro drew a sharp breath
and swivelled to stand right in front of her again.
'You understand nothing, Queen Jade. Not a damn
thing.'

'Enlighten me, then.'

He pressed his fists against the wall either side
of her head and stared into her eyes. 'I can't sleep
with a woman who's going to marry another man.'

'Surely most of the women you meet are going
to marry another man some time,' she argued.
'Are you the marrying type yourself?'

He froze. 'No.'

No. She didn't think so. He had that air of the
loner about him—the distant leader who inspired
huge loyalty but remained isolated… Yes, she understood his type very well.

'We've already established that *if* I ever get
married, it's not going to be a normal one. I'll do
what I'm expected to do, at the time I'm required
to. But what I do with my body *before* then? I

want to lose my virginity to someone I actually *want*. At a place and time of my choosing. *All* of these things are *my* choices.'

He still loomed over her and his voice was a thread of steel. 'And are you saying your choice for all that is *me*?'

It was impossible not to answer him honestly when he was right before her, gazing right at her, seeing right through her. But asking? She was suddenly so afraid of his answer.

'Obviously you don't have to,' she muttered helplessly. 'I can't order you. I am not *your* queen. And I apologise if I misinterpreted your interest. As we've already established, I'm not especially experienced in such things.'

His jaw slackened for a few seconds and then he smiled. 'In "such things"?'

She'd just propositioned a man she barely *knew*. What on earth had come over her? 'If you'll excuse me, I'll go—'

'No. I won't excuse you.' He leaned closer. 'Won't let you leave.' He gazed down at her. 'Not yet.'

But he didn't kiss her as she wanted him to, and his fierce expression didn't lighten. In fact, the longer the silence grew, the more remote his expression became.

Her breathing quickened as every doubt mushroomed. She was so embarrassed. She never should have said anything. Never should have wanted.

'I apologise,' she muttered in an agonised whisper. 'I shouldn't have wanted—'

His harsh inhalation silenced her. 'You shouldn't apologise for wanting someone.'

She could feel that horrible blush burning across her skin. Worse was the horrible feeling rotting inside. Regret.

But then he smiled. 'You do realise you've invited a tiger in, don't you? Hell, Jade.' He breathed out. 'You must know I wouldn't mind if you ordered me to do what you really want.'

Her mouth dried and she just gazed up at him, unable to say another thing. All courage stolen by the promise in his eyes.

He lifted a hand from the wall beside her and lifted that lock of her hair again. 'You know what you need?'

She shook her head mutely.

'Food.'

Startled, she giggled.

'I'm serious.' But he grinned at her, transforming into a teasing, good-humoured hunk. 'You can't make important decisions on an empty stomach. And I've been watching—you've only had a couple of coffees and one sandwich from the lunch platters I specially ordered. I'm hungry on your behalf.'

Was it wrong to be pleased that he'd been watching?

'I'm starving,' she admitted.

'Then why the hell aren't you exploring all the cafés in the neighbourhood? Isn't that the point of this stupid switch? So you get to eat corndogs from street vendors?'

Now he knew, she couldn't help confessing everything to him. 'I don't even know what a corndog is.'

'What?'

'And I can't get Juno's money card to work.'

'You *what*?'

'I don't have any cash.' She tried to laugh about it. 'Never have. I know that's ridiculously precious, but—'

'You don't have any money.' He wasn't smiling any more. 'And there's no food in the apartment. Why didn't you *say* something?'

'I didn't want to bother Juno. I wanted to manage alone—without assistants and security...'

'What about a friend?' He pushed back from the wall, dropping his arms so she was free. 'Come on.'

'Where to?' She almost had to run to keep up with him.

'To get the best meal in Manhattan.'

He didn't look at her as he repeatedly pressed the button to summon the elevator.

'Don't you need a jacket?' she asked.

'Oh, no,' he said. 'I could do with the cold air.'

A minute later he guided her out onto the street; glancing down, he led her swiftly along the pavement. Less than five minutes later he ushered her into a tiny pizza parlour in a side street just down from the office building.

'Is this the best meal to be had in New York?' Amusement bubbled out of her.

'There are so many meals. But when you're starving, this is a good one to start with. Plus, it's fast.'

'It needs to be fast?' Her heart raced.

'It does.'

He ordered a couple of enormous slices of pizza. There weren't table or chairs for them to sit at, so instead they slowly walked back to the office and ate on the way. Jade smiled as she licked her finger. She wasn't just breaking every palace etiquette rule, she was throwing caution completely to the wind.

'Good?'

So good, she couldn't reply, her mouth was too full.

His sudden smile was so stunning she couldn't have spoken anyway.

'I am so damn glad I am not your employer,' he muttered beneath his breath.

She swallowed and grinned impishly at him. 'So I shouldn't call you *Boss*?'

'Absolutely not.'

She chuckled.

'But I am going to advance you Juno's pay,' he said. 'In cash.'

'I don't want—'

'Consider it a loan. You know you need money for food and to do things,' he interrupted bluntly. 'Don't worry, I have the feeling you're good for it.'

She was. But she truly appreciated the offer. 'Thank you, that's very kind of you.'

He shot her a sardonic smile and half bowed. 'It's my pleasure, Your Highness.'

She winced inside. 'Don't…'

'Then don't "polite me" off.'

'It was basic manners, nothing fancy,' she said defensively. 'Boss.'

There was a pregnant pause in which she wondered just what he was about to do. Every cell overflowed with anticipation.

To her disappointment, he just huffed out a tense growl.

'Come on, I've ordered you a car.' He nodded towards the black sedan now waiting outside his building. 'I'm not driving you. Not tonight.'

Crushed, Jade almost stumbled. So he'd declined her other—unmentionable—invitation? Given her some pizza to soften the blow?

But then he took her hand in his. 'We can have one night, if that's really what you want.'

'One?' Her heart leapt.

'Neither of us need complicated.'

'So we don't see each other after?' She nodded. 'That's good.'

His eyes widened slightly, then narrowed. 'So to clarify, we're going to have a one-night stand in which we do almost every possible carnal act, including you giving me your virginity, and then we'll never see each other again.'

His blunt description of the plan scorched her sensibility, leaving her with nothing left but excitement and acquiescence. 'Yes... I...you...'

She couldn't finish. Couldn't articulate what it was she wanted him to give her. It felt, not forbidden, but too *greedy*.

'Yes,' he confirmed. 'You do. I do. We do.' He rolled his shoulders and walked her nearer to that waiting car. 'You've finished that report, right? So don't come in tomorrow. Take the day. Then I'll pick you up and we'll have dinner.'

'We just had dinner.'

He brushed her hair back from her face, letting his fingers linger on her jaw as he did. 'We'll have another dinner. Most people need them every day.'

Heat swept over her again at the light caress and she couldn't resist turning to the slight cup of his hand. 'You don't want to just—'

He stroked her jaw gently but the blaze in his eyes was all erotic warning. 'I'm not settling for anything less than a *whole* night with you, Jade. Start to finish. I want drinks and dancing and privacy and all the hours there can possibly be in one damned night.'

Her legs trembled. 'Where?' She swallowed nervously. Drinks and dancing could mean cameras. There could be cameras even now and she'd been so mesmerised by him she hadn't even *thought* of them.

'My place,' he answered swiftly and released her. 'But now you leave. Now you have the rest of this night to decide if this is what you really want. You need to be sure, Jade. And I'm not touching you again because if I do…' He drew in a sharp breath.

The sensations swirling deep within her now were so hot and exciting…how was she supposed to wait? But her training—that insistence upon emotional control—finally came to her aid.

'Okay.' She stepped away from him.

'Tomorrow, I'll come and you'll either get into my car, or you won't. Let me know your final decision then.'

Her mouth dried at a horrible thought and she quickly turned back. 'What if you change *your* mind?'

CHAPTER SIX

AS IF HE would ever change his mind?

At work the next morning Alvaro tried to stay so busy he didn't have a second to think. It didn't work. The only thing going round in his head was *Jade*.

Jade the tempting. Jade the innocent. Jade the literal freaking *queen*.

Jade, who lived on the other side of an enormous ocean, who had endless responsibilities, obligations and duties that he would never really understand, and who faced intensely unique, challenging pressures. No wonder she wanted her three weeks of freedom.

She'd embarked on a totally crazy caper with her sister, risking so much if either of them got caught. Yet she'd wasted almost a full week of it struggling to succeed in something she knew little about, to save her sister's job. Chancing discovery to an even more massive extent. No wonder she'd plugged in her headphones and stared into that computer screen for hours. And she'd pulled it off…until the moment she'd blurted the truth to him.

Jade not Juno. Stranger instead of employee.

The relief had been intense, before the uncontrollable urge had slammed into him and stolen his reason. He'd barely slept last night, his brain kept wildly awake by the constant recollection of those frantic few moments in the office and the resulting tension in his body.

Her confession. His kiss. Her killer response.

He hadn't given her the tender first-time kiss she should've had—that he would've given her if he'd known. He'd been so wound up he'd lost it the second he'd realised they weren't bound by workplace restrictions. He hadn't just unleashed, he'd all but lost his mind as he'd done what he'd wanted to do for days—kissed her to total satisfaction, subduing the desire that had been straining between them both since they'd first clashed last Monday morning…while stoking it higher at the same time. Their chemistry hadn't just been combustible, it had become an out-of-control inferno in seconds.

Then her second confession—of such complete innocence? And her barely whispered request for him to help her with that?

Yeah, his eyes had been wide, wide open for hours.

Because this was wrong. So wrong. Wasn't this worse than sleeping with an employee? To seduce a virgin queen—didn't that go against every one of his own rules?

No drama, remember? Certainly, no *dreams*...

He'd needed to get away from her. Not only to ensure her certainty and his own, but to prepare himself for the pure torture of her—he knew her gorgeously eager body would devastate his.

Not going to do that. Not going to rush this, or rush *her*.

He should've said no. But never had anything been as impossible as saying no to Queen Jade Monroyale. But while he couldn't resist, he could control the event and its outcome. He wanted it to be good for her and he was arrogant enough to believe he could make it so. He'd felt her shaking in his arms, he'd heard her moan in pleasure and felt her restless movements as she'd sought more...

It seemed her life had been almost completely prescribed, but she was mostly happy to go along with that. Even insisting she would eventually marry whomever was the best political match for her country. Irritation flared the length of his spine. He loathed that idea—which was ironic, because he never gave the idea of marriage a thought. It wasn't for him and wouldn't ever be. He valued his independence too much. So she was right, who she chose to marry later on was no concern of his. At all.

He gritted his teeth. She wanted what she wanted with whom she wanted. And frankly he was absurdly privileged to be her pick. He knew this wasn't simply opportunity. She could have found other times, other ways, other men, if she'd so wanted—she'd proven herself a resourceful survivor at heart—but until now, she hadn't wanted to.

So who was he to deny her all she wanted in her few weeks of freedom? Or say whether she should or shouldn't? Especially when he badly wanted the exact same thing?

He paced through the office, wishing time would speed up as long as it then slowed down once he got to her. He picked up a copy of the free daily paper that someone had left in the chill-out area. The international section slid out—the second he saw the lead picture, he knew why. For there 'she' was. 'Queen Jade' with King Leonardo—monarchs of the neighbouring nations of Monrova and Severene. They were dancing together at the Monrova Winter Ball, Juno looking up at the King while he was as intently focused on her.

Alvaro studied the image closely, seeking to spot the differences between the sisters. Juno's hair was tied up, masking the shortened length, and her face was slightly fuller, her smile wide, her skin a touch more bronzed. The real Jade appeared slightly more physically fragile than this. Yet she wasn't weak. She was strong and controlled and very determined. But she was also lonely. He recognised her isolation and her raw need for physical connection reverberated someplace deep within him.

He felt it too. It was exactly why he couldn't deny her. It was also exactly why he *should*.

One night. What harm could come from one night?

He glanced at King Leonardo again and his hackles rose. That was not a man who'd ever be willing to commit to a sexless marriage. Frankly Alvaro didn't know anyone who would—male or female. Jade shouldn't be so glib about making such a sacrifice either.

But the way Leonardo was looking at the woman he was dancing with? Alvaro tensed. Did the King know this *wasn't* Jade?

In the end he sent the remaining office staff home early. It was Christmas after all.

It was a little after five when he leaned against the car, eyeing her apartment building and pretending he was chilled. As if. He'd sent the text two minutes ago. Would she reply in person or by phone? Yes or no? The door opened. He folded his arms tightly across his chest because it was the only way to hold himself back as she walked towards him. She'd left her hair loose and now he saw just how stunningly long it was. It hung in a gleaming sweep of loose chestnut curls all the way to her waist. His jaw dropped yet every muscle tightened. Her green eyes were usually backlit by a banked fire, but the smoulder in them now sucked all moisture from his mouth. It was as if he'd swallowed sandpaper. Her smile was shy, but her lips were glossed and pillowy and he wanted a first kiss do-over. Her black dress wasn't slinky, but demurely fitted—belted at the waist only to flare and finish mid-calf. It was sexier than any he'd seen. Those stupidly thin high-heeled shoes were on her feet again and she'd slung a black leather jacket over her arm and he could no longer breathe.

'Is everything okay?' she asked.

It took him a moment to realise she'd paused a couple of paces away and was watching him warily. Apparently, time had stopped for him but not for her, and he'd been staring in silence for too long. Yet even now he wasn't able to speak. His tongue was sealed to the roof of his mouth and his throat was so tight it hurt to nod. He straightened and had to consciously tell his arms to unfold so he could open the damn car door.

'Shall I get in?' Colour washed across her fine features, but a small knowing smile curved her luscious lips.

Vixen.

He pulled away the second she'd fastened her seat belt. That soft vanilla had arrived with her and he struggled to steady his breathing.

'Was your day okay?' she asked softly.

'They missed you,' he croaked, trying to think

of normal things. He belatedly realised he'd not given her the chance to say goodbye to them even though they had no idea she wasn't Juno and wasn't coming back after the Christmas break. But no doubt she met people all the time, mostly briefly, with no permanency or long-term relationship ever developing. He was just another person to pass through her life too.

'What did you do today?' he asked, distracting himself from the unwelcome sensation at that thought.

'I went for a walk...'

As she trailed off he glanced and registered how tense she was too. Instinctively he reached out and covered her tight fist with his hand. A sizzle zinged up his arm at the small contact, but she tensed beneath his hold and he immediately loosened his grip. But she didn't pull away, instead she flipped her fingers and laced them through his. Alvaro had never held hands with anyone. Ever. But for the first time all day he felt as if he could breathe.

'I'm really glad you came for me,' she said softly.

Alvaro's gut clenched as that too-sweet sentiment plunged him into a vat of scalding oil—the images her words conjured up were too graphic, too inappropriate. He needed to rein in his own sexual impulse around her, because she'd not meant that double-entendre. She was too inexperienced and this night was such folly. But he couldn't force himself to turn the car around. He simply couldn't stop.

'I wasn't sure what to wear.'

She could've worn a sack, she'd look stunning regardless. But he did love this outfit, he did love the fact that she'd thought about what to wear for him. But his customary facility with compliments had fled. Hell, his whole brain seemed to have blown.

The relief when he pulled into the basement of his building was immense, but he could still barely speak as he led her into the elevator and keyed in the code to unlock access to the penthouse. He tossed his keys and wallet onto the nearest small table and breathed deeply.

'You have amazing views up here.' She walked through to the large lounge.

The penthouse overlooked the Hudson River, but she'd turned her back on the vast windows and was studying the apartment itself. Her avid curiosity made him smile.

'What does the décor tell you?' He relaxed enough to tease her. 'Any insights you can glean about me from the room?'

That colour washed back into her cheeks and she touched her tongue to her lips in an unconsciously nervous, yet provocative gesture that made him harder than he'd been in his life. But it was imperative he go slow. That he give her every chance to change her mind. Hell, *he* still wasn't anywhere near sure this was a good idea.

'It does tell me a few things, actually.' Her smile was suddenly impish.

'Oh?' He stilled. 'Such as?'

'You like comfort.' Her smile widened as she ran her hand over the soft woollen throw on the arm of his massive plush sofa. 'You're a sensualist, for all your outward discipline.'

Heat pooled in his already aching body. Because—at least as far as she was concerned—she was right.

'What would the palace tell me about you?' he asked huskily.

'It would tell you everything about my family going back eight hundred years or so. Before then, there was a fire and we lost those very valuable records. But the art and antiques collection that has been amassed over the centuries is amazing.'

'But what about your room?' he pressed, keen to know something more of her. 'Do you not get to choose your own pink fluffy cushions Princess Palace-Style?'

'Never,' she giggled. 'That wouldn't do. The décor has remained mostly the same for ever.'

But wasn't she the Queen? Didn't she get to dictate—demand fulfilment of her every whim?

'That's a shame,' he commiserated lightly. 'You should get to choose your own cushions. I like cushions.'

'I can tell.' She laughed as she gazed at the plump pile of them on one low shelf.

'Home should be welcoming,' he said, unafraid to admit it.

'Well, I don't know that you could call Monrova palace *welcoming*. I mean, it is amazing and stunning and beautiful but—'

'Not very comfortable?' He frowned. 'If everything is ancient, won't the seats be too small? Doorways too low?'

'Oh, the doorways were built for giants, but that has meant it's been challenging to heat.' She ventured deeper into his lounge, studying the spines of the books lining the shelves. She paused at one point. 'Is this your mother?' she asked.

Of course, she'd spotted his one personal photo in the whole penthouse.

'I don't have a mother,' he said.

She turned to face him. '*Everyone* has a mother,' she said gently. 'It's basic biology.'

'Biology?' he echoed. Then he could keep this straightforward and factual. 'Okay, there was the woman who gave birth to me. Then there was the woman who supposedly adopted me. And then there was the woman who saved me. Which would you say is my *mother*?' He couldn't help the bitterness in his tone.

And when he summoned the courage to look directly at her, he saw her jade eyes glimmering with an emotion he didn't want to identify.

'The one who saved you,' she said.

She was right, of course. The nearest he'd had to a mother. The woman he owed everything. Alvaro never discussed his personal life or background. But he understood Jade's curiosity because he felt the same about her. So for once he offered just a little.

'Her name is Ellen.' His gaze rested on the photo briefly and he couldn't help a small smile because Ellen *hated* that picture. 'She's still alive and I see her regularly.' He looked back to Jade, but her eyes were still filled with soft compassion. 'Come on,' he growled and strode through to the open-plan kitchen.

'You're cooking?' Jade studied the preparations he already had under way on the large wooden bench.

'I'm fairly competent,' he teased at her surprise. 'Are you willing to risk it?'

'Of course,' she rushed to answer with that cut-glass courtesy, but that delicious flush swarmed her cheeks again. 'Thank you for going to the trouble.'

'I don't think cooking is the trouble here,' he muttered, barely holding himself together. She got to him in ways other than the one he expected. 'Do you think we can be civilised for a few more minutes?'

'Is that what we're trying to do?'

'Yes.'

'Why?'

Oh, she was going to be the absolute death of him. He braced both hands on the bench and let out a helpless laugh. 'Given I know how rubbish you are at keeping regular meals when left to your own devices, I don't want you running out of energy any time soon.'

'So, it's purely for biological reasons?'

'No,' he growled. 'It's because you need time to be sure.'

'I wouldn't be here if I wasn't,' she replied with determined ease. 'It's only...'

'Sex?'

That colour stormed into her cheeks.

He gazed at her, grappling with his conscience. That was how he'd always thought of it, but he wasn't sure that *this* time it was. He didn't feel guilty about taking what she was offering, but he wanted it to be *better* than 'only sex' for her.

Suddenly he couldn't resist touching her. He walked over and lifted her chin with just a finger. She tilted instantly, willing and welcome. Slowly he pressed his lips to hers in a tentative, gentle touch—truly first-kiss-worthy. Her response was instant. Her soft, sweet mouth surprisingly mobile, she teased him back and made him forget about first kiss anything. She knew what she wanted and he wanted it too. He'd always worked like a dog until he got it. So he'd do the same now. And there was *nothing* he wanted more in the world in this instant than Jade Monroyale's total satisfaction.

But as she moaned, he broke the kiss and made himself step back to the bench.

She stared at him—her green eyes gleamed like jewels lit by an inner flame. And her expression was ever so slightly resentful.

'Food first, remember?' But his voice was hoarse and his resolve weak and he was a little too glad she felt this need as keenly as she did.

'Can I help you at all?' she asked after a moment.

He pressed his hands back on the bench, desperate to regain focus and not drag her straight to bed. 'Do you cook in the palace?'

'No,' she confessed with an adorably guilty smile. 'It wasn't considered a necessary part of my education, which I know is terrible. It's a life skill.'

'That it is.' He picked up the knife and took his frustration out on the herbs.

'Whereas you were obviously taught well.'

Actually, he was self-taught. It had been that or go hungry. But he wasn't giving her any more of his sob story. 'Can you grab a couple of tomatoes from the pantry?' He aimed for diversion.

'Of course.'

Her heard her opening a couple of doors behind him and glanced back. She'd paused in front of the pantry and was taking in the well-stocked, perfectly ordered shelves. 'You live alone, right?' she asked.

And this was why he rarely had house guests— why he didn't open the cupboards to anyone, so to speak. Because it only invited questions he had no desire to answer. 'Always.'

She nodded but her eyes were wide.

'I imagine your palace pantry is far better stocked,' he pointed out dryly. 'But from the sounds of things, you wouldn't know.'

'I admit I wouldn't.' She reached for a couple of tomatoes and gave the pantry a final glance before closing the door.

'Cooking is a stress release for me. Plus, you know I need a bit of feeding.' He paused; he never explained himself to anyone but somehow a sliver of truth escaped. 'But I can't bear the thought of not having food in the house because endless hunger is a vivid memory that, unfortunately, I can't forget.'

She faced him. 'I'm sorry you suffered that.'

For a second the emotion that cascaded through him was almost too strong to contain. He was glad he had to concentrate on the searing-hot grill.

'Do you think you can you manage to open a bottle of wine?' he asked, unable to look up from the hot plate and into her eyes. He needed anything to divert them from this moment.

'Of course.'

She chose a bottle and poured two glasses from

it, taking a seat at the table from which to watch him as he sizzled two steaks on the grill. With the herbs and tomatoes, the salad he'd begun earlier was now complete. Fresh and simple.

'Shall we eat in here?' He took the chair opposite the one she'd taken.

She stared at the plates with admiration. 'It looks amazing.'

'And yet you're not eating.' He sent her a laughing glance. 'You need fuel or you're not going to survive the night.'

'Not *survive*?'

Her laughter bubbled but at the same time he saw anticipation light her face. She was curious, his petite queen. And hungry.

'You don't think I'm serious?' he teased.

'Perhaps I have more stamina than you give me credit for.' She spoke with such regal preciseness, but it was pure challenge and they both knew it.

'Oh, you do?' He attacked his steak with the fierce passion he was trying to stop himself using on her.

'Yes, I do. I might not feel the need to work out every morning and night like you, but I do exercise. And I do—generally—eat well, and rest.' She glared at his smothered snort. 'I think I'm fit enough to handle you.'

Happily, it wouldn't be long 'til he found out. He just had to hang onto his sanity long enough to make it good for her. 'I think you should stop talking and start eating.'

She loaded up her fork and tasted the salad, briefly closing her eyes as she did. 'You want all the feedback, don't you?'

'Damn right I do.'

'It's good.' She took in a breath. 'It's better than good.'

'It's fresh produce,' he demurred. 'Can't really screw it up. So, come on, what exercise do you prefer?'

She lifted her nose primly. 'I endure a variety of activities. Treadmill. Circuit. Laps of the pool. Gymnastics.'

'You *endure* them?'

'I've never really got that endorphin high,' she admitted. 'I blame my trainer—she's a dragon.'

'You have a female drill sergeant?'

'Well, it was never going to be a *guy*.' Jade laughed but that blush battled its way back into her cheeks. 'My father would never have allowed that.'

'He was that strict? You had no men around you at all?'

'In a way it was good—they were aspirational figures, right? My old governess was a former university professor. My trainer is just in cahoots with the palace physician. They conspire to make life hell.'

'You're the Queen, Jade, can't you just tell them to leave you alone?'

'There are expectations I must meet. It is part of my duty. Spent so long training for it—language lessons, politics, history, philosophy, ethics, manners, meditation and a boring exercise regime.'

'Meditation?'

'To master emotions.'

Wow. What a regimented, prescribed life.

'Don't feel sorry for me.' She smiled at him. 'I was a privileged princess through and through. Thoroughly spoilt.'

He wasn't entirely sure he believed her.

'Anyway, they're right. I need to exercise more.' She grimaced. 'The crown is too heavy. It doesn't sit right.'

'You don't believe you can hold its weight? Because you can,' he said reassuringly. 'I saw you single-handedly disarm thousands of angry emails. Trust me, you can handle the crown.'

Her mouth hung open for a second and then she smiled and blushed concurrently. 'No, I mean it's literally too heavy. It weighs a tonne. Gives me a headache five minutes after I put it on.'

Oh. He laughed. But he'd meant what he'd said. 'Have a new one made. I'm sure you can afford it.'

'I couldn't do that.' She stared at him in amazement. 'It's a *tradition.*'

'Make a new tradition.' He shrugged.

'You make it sound so easy.'

'That's because it is easy. Just choose what you want. Say it. Do it.'

'Is that what you did? Was it all that easy for you?'

He paused. 'I came from a position of far less power and privilege than you, Jade. So no, some things were most definitely not easy. But in a way, I had more liberty to do what I wanted. Because no one knew and no one gave a damn and no one was ever going to try and help me or require me to do something "their" way.'

'I'm sorry, I didn't mean to be—'

'Don't apologise, I'm glad you didn't face the struggles I did.'

'So how did you overcome them?' she asked. 'How did you do it all alone?'

She was so genuinely curious, he found himself telling her a snippet of history he'd not mentioned in years. 'My first plan to gain financial freedom was to be a professional sportsman. It didn't matter to me which sport—I'd got a full ride through sport into a good school. I was captain of both basketball and football teams and I'd decided to do whichever paid me more to get through college. I trained my ass off. But I tore the muscles in my knee and that ended that. No more captain. No more sports teams. No more school.'

She looked shocked. 'They took away your scholarship?'

He nodded. 'I was a nerd as much as I was a jock, but they wanted me for physique, not physics.' He shrugged. 'I don't know why, but math just came easy and I had ideas and I sure as hell had nothing to lose. Only my own time. So, working around a bunch of hand-to-mouth jobs, I developed that fitness app. It grew very popular, very quickly. I leveraged it while hustling other work on the side, earning however I could, investing in small, then larger projects. There was a lot of luck and timing.'

'And effort.'

'Sure.' Maximum effort, all hours and every weekend for years. Hell, he still worked more hours than not.

'I can't imagine being the CEO of a huge conglomerate.'

He laughed. 'Yes, but a CEO of a private company can be directive and bossy and not give a damn about what other people think. I can't imagine what it would be like being Queen of a country where you're like public property. A figurehead, a role model who everyone looks to for guidance on everything from fashion to foreign affairs.'

'There's a parliament, my people vote. I don't make all the rules myself.'

It sounded to him as if she didn't make any. 'And you get a Sovereign Grant, I know. But you still give official assent, right? You're still the overseer of good governance.'

Jade had spent her life being trained to understand good governance. To understand *being* good, full stop.

'Do you have good advisors?'

'They're very experienced,' Jade murmured evasively and took the last bite of the tender meat.

'And they want you to marry that Leonardo guy.'

She shot him a glance.

'It must've been hard to be separated from your mother and your sister,' he added. 'Even with all your women mentors, you must have missed them.'

'Juno and I stayed in touch as best we could. She visited each year for a while...' But then Juno and their father had fought and Juno had left. 'Juno hasn't been back in years, not 'til now.'

'What about your mother?'

'I never saw her again after their divorce.'

His eyes widened. 'You were how old?'

'Eight.'

He looked at a loss. 'Pretty harsh way to deal with a difficult situation.'

His quiet response made her chest ache. She never discussed this, but Alvaro had got under her guard.

'My father didn't want to put in the work to find a new way of working as a separated family. He just cut her out, like a cancer or something.' It had devastated Jade and she knew it had been even harder on Juno. 'He was so rigid, he refused to even consider—'

She tried to catch back the fear and the pain it had caused her, wanting to shove it back down deep. Thinking about this was pointless; there was no changing it.

'I know he was hurt too,' she muttered. 'Badly. That's why he reacted so harshly, but…'

She shook her head. She'd *never* shared this. She couldn't trust anyone—that had been drilled into her.

'Why didn't it work out for your parents, do you know?'

'Maybe because she wasn't a princess?' Jade said sadly. 'She was Hollywood royalty, so she was used to some similar pressure… But I think maybe they were too different. And too quick to rush into it.'

'Is that why you think some arranged marriage with a prince would be better for you?'

'I…' She stared at him, her breath stolen. But then she lifted her chin. 'Maybe. I think my country deserves stability within the Crown.'

'Your country deserves that?' He watched her. 'What do *you* deserve?'

'My few weeks of freedom,' she said softly. 'And then?' She shrugged. She didn't want to think about it any more. Not tonight. 'Every family has its quirks, right?' she muttered glibly.

Alvaro's smile twisted. 'My family is a doozy,' he offered, as if recognising her regret at revealing any of this. 'I got some of that "cut-you-out-like-a-cancer" treatment too.'

The woman who gave birth to me...the woman who supposedly adopted me...

What did that mean, 'supposedly'? And was that when he'd been afraid he wouldn't have enough to eat? Had he not just gone hungry, but been starved of all those other necessities too?

'I'm sorry, Alvaro.'

He closed his eyes momentarily. 'What is it you're doing here, Jade?'

One truth spilled. 'Not having people watch my every move. Or have cameras trained on me every time I leave my home. I'm eating all the cheap chocolate. Soaking up the bright Christmas lights.'

'You don't have Christmas lights in Monrova?'

'They're very refined fairy lights. Traditional and dignified.'

'You want neon party lights?' He half smiled.

'Glow-in-the-dark reindeer? Yes, I do. Why not?'

'Surely as Queen you can make your own Christmas traditions? Demand all the fluorescence you can stand?'

One might think so, but it wasn't that easy.

Alvaro's expression grew serious again. 'What are you really doing *here*, Jade?'

She swallowed. 'I don't know,' she admitted from the bottom of her heart. 'I just know there's nowhere else I want to be right now.' She didn't know why she was whispering, but she couldn't seem to breathe any volume into her voice.

'Me neither.' He reached out to caress her cheek, sliding his hand to cup her jaw. 'But you know this is madness.'

'It's my time for madness.' But her heart puckered at the swirl of emotion clouding his eyes. 'You're not doing this out of pity, are you?'

'Pity?' He half choked. 'No. Not pity.'

'You'll have a good time too? It's not all about pleasing me, is it?'

'Why shouldn't it be?'

'People try to please me all the time. It can be awkward. They don't quite know how to act around me. They get nervous and it's... I don't want this to be like that.'

'Not going to lie, I'm a little nervous, Jade. I don't want to hurt you and I do want you to have a good time. But honestly, I'm being more selfish now than I've ever been in my life. And I'm a pretty selfish guy.'

She didn't believe that about him.

'But I'm not awkward around you. And I think we're past getting hung up on our respective jobs and titles.'

'No one's ever yelled at me the way you did the other morning,' she confessed with a wry smile.

'And you snapped right back, which, I admit, doesn't usually happen to me. But I'm guessing you don't usually do that?'

'Not usually, no,' she acknowledged. 'It would be rude and abusive of my position. I know I have more power than most people, I need to be mindful of that.'

'Not with me. Not then. Certainly not now. I'm not awed by your crown, Jade.'

'I know you're not.' She half laughed.

'I'm glad you're not too polite to yell at me. I don't want you to be polite or hold back from me in any way. Not at any time. Understand?' He stepped closer and she battled to stand in place. 'So if you don't usually, if you master your emotions, why did you yell at me? Why did you lose your cool?'

'Because I was tired, and you were half naked, and I couldn't get my brain to work.'

'So to get absolute honesty from you, I just need to strip down and wear you out?'

His smile lifted and all she could do was stare at him. It was impossible, how beautiful he was. And she realised, with slight shock, that he could do anything he wanted with her.

'I'm going to make love to you, Jade.'

His rough, low promise devastated her.

She swallowed hard. 'I thought we were having sex.'

He shook his head and the serious determination in his eyes melted the last of her mind. 'If this is the one night that you get, with a man you actually want, and who you're giving your virginity to, then you deserve to be worshipped and adored. You deserve to have the best possible experience. So no, we're not having sex. I'm making love to you.' He stood up from the table and held his hand out to her. 'Okay?'

She couldn't possibly speak now. But she put her hand in his and rose to meet him.

'Jade?'

She was trembling. Aching so much for his touch. The kiss was everything she needed. A luscious sweep of passion and security. She slung her arms around his neck and heard his pleased little grunt as he caught her. He stepped her back until she was braced against the kitchen wall. She loved it like this with him so big before her.

'Jade?' He pulled back to look into her eyes. 'I want to know what you're thinking, what you're feeling, whether you're okay. I need to know that, sweetheart.'

But as he spoke, he worked the buttons down the front of her dress free and pushed it from her shoulders, leaving her in just her green silk slip. He fingered the thin straps on her shoulders, tracing one down to the seam at the neckline, and looked. His smile made her so grateful for the support of the wall behind her. 'Why, Queen Jade,' he mock-reproved. 'I do believe you're not wearing a bra.'

She laughed, finally able to answer. 'It's hard enough to breathe around you,' she muttered. 'I didn't want anything constricting my ribs and making it even harder.'

His gaze shot to her face again and he seemed oddly touched. 'You know you can say "when" any time.'

'That doesn't seem fair,' she breathed.

'Life isn't always fair. I think you and I both know that already.'

She didn't want to think about that right now. She lifted her chin and pressed her full, pulsing lips to his again. Her toes curled in her shoes when he kissed her back. His hands shaped her curves beneath the silk, eventually sliding under the hem and up to the lacy panties she'd specially worn. She gasped as he grazed the strip of silk at the front.

'I'm a big guy, sweetheart, you need to be ready,' he said softly as he kissed down her neck and across her collarbones. 'Getting you there is my job now.'

A wave of anticipation swamped her and she moaned as he skated his fingers across the dampened silk again.

His little laugh was low and searing. 'You like that idea?' He growled and nipped her gently. 'Do you want to know just how big?'

'Yes,' she breathed. She wanted to know everything about him. And she ached to feel *all* of him.

But her eyes closed and she could only lean against the wall for support as he skimmed over her secret parts. And as he kissed her deeply she unashamedly drove her hips against the sinfully tormenting touch of his hand.

'Please,' she begged but he kept strumming her so lightly, while his hot mouth softly kissed her sensitive skin and breathed even hotter words against her.

'You want me inside you, Jade?'

'Yes.' Desperately. So desperately. But he still didn't press harder where she wanted him to. And it was deliberate. The man was an impossible tease.

'We have all night,' he promised.

'That's…not…long,' she breathlessly complained, pressing harder against his wicked hand.

'One night is made up of many, many moments.' He finally flicked his fingers that touch harder. 'And this is a moment now, sweetheart. Take it.'

She slammed her hands on his broad biceps for balance, crying out as the orgasm shuddered through her—leaving her body so weak she couldn't stand.

Alvaro swiftly picked her up and carried her from the kitchen. She revelled in the heat of his chest and the ripple of his muscles against her as he strode with leashed purpose. She took in sharp details, like snaps captured in millisecond moments. Cotton and comfort, white linen contrasted with grey walls and heavy curtains, woollen rugs on wooden floors. Lit by the only lamp on a table beside his bed, his bedroom was large and sumptuous. She wasn't surprised by that this time; his whole apartment revealed a predilection for sumptuousness. Of his enjoyment for plush, soft furnishings. Like a caveman's den filled with soft skins—all for warmth and safety and sensuality.

He placed her on the bed, bunched the hem of her emerald slip and lifted it. She lifted her arms and it was gone in a second. Then he pushed her onto her back and slid her panties down her legs, then the shoes from her feet, so at last she was naked on his bed.

He sucked in a breath with a hiss. 'Do you know what I am awed by, Jade?'

She shook her head.

'You. Like this.'

Before she could reply he kissed her—brought his body on hers. For the first time she felt the weight of him and it was so, so good as he ground her into the mattress beneath that she cried out.

'Soon,' he promised. 'Soon, sweetheart.'

But he pulled back to only straddle her. Tenderly he cupped her breasts in his big hands, teasing her taut nipples and laughing when she became breathless all over again. He took his time. Gentle, not so gentle, gentle again. The teasing licks of his fingers, hands and lips were like waves creeping further up the shore of her arousal. That sensation grew closer. That desperation a deeper ache within. This time it wasn't his finger teasing her sensitive, private place. It was his tongue.

She shivered, her knees instinctively rising because this was so personal, so intimate. 'Alvaro…'

'Let me,' he rasped.

And she couldn't resist the carnal plea in his voice, not when it echoed her own so completely. Her legs splayed and her reward was the slide not just of his tongue, but of his fingers again. Only this time, this time, he pushed one inside her. She gasped and then breathed for more.

'You're so tight, sweetheart,' he growled.

She lay, stunned to stillness as she adjusted to the sensation of having someone so intimate with her, doing *that*. 'Alvaro…'

'I like the taste of you, Jade. I like all of you.'

Heat and delight burnished her entire body, because his words felt more than merely playful. Slowly he worked, in and out and again and again as he softly licked her most sensitive point with relentlessly gentle stokes. Inexorably, his focused care overcame her self-consciousness and the sensations tumbled faster and faster and faster within until she totally tensed. Her hands spread wide and she gripped the sheet. She drew so taut, her hips arched high off the bed. Yet still he plundered and tasted and utterly tormented her until suddenly all she could do was scream.

Endless, timeless moments later the orgasm left her limp and devastated in a splayed heap in the middle of his bed. Yet despite that overwhelming pleasure, she still yearned inside. She still *ached*. Because she wanted all of him and now she could barely move.

'Alvaro,' she called to him with a plaintive moan.

'I'm here.' But he stood back from the bed. For a moment he just looked at her, that satisfied twist still on his lips as he blatantly studied her pinkened parts from where the rub of his fingers and the rasp of his stubble had gently scoured her skin.

His muscles bunched. Her mouth dried and she propped herself up on her elbows to watch with fascination as he slowly stripped for her. First his shirt. And it wasn't only her appetite returning, it was her energy too. And he knew. He knew as he maintained that teasing eye contact and slowly unfastened his belt. Jade's breath stalled in her lungs as he undid the button of his trousers, half laughing as he had to do a shimmy of his hips to release the zipper given the strain it was under. But Jade could only then stare at the muscular thighs he'd just revealed. She dragged her gaze back up but only made it as far as his black knit boxers. He stepped closer to the bed and reached for something on the table. She watched as he slowly rolled the condom down the straining, rigid length of him. She swallowed and unconsciously rubbed her hands down her tense thighs.

'Do you want to touch me?' His voice was hoarse.

Somehow she was kneeling up on the mattress. She'd not even realised she'd moved. And she'd certainly not realised she was audibly panting. But she didn't care any more. The exhaustion from those earlier orgasms was obliterated by the yearning raging through her blood now. She wanted to touch him, to taste him, to test him. She wanted to discover everything she could—about him, with him.

He didn't move as she reached out. Indeed, he seemed to be braced, his feet planted wide apart, his magnificent body strained to take her touch. His jaw clamped but a groan escaped regardless as she bravely planted both palms on his broad chest and began a slow sweep of pure, fascinated inspection. He flinched beneath her touch. She felt the heat, the rise of sweat in his body.

'You said you were big,' she breathed. 'You're also beautiful.' And there was a dampness between her legs, an excitement in her pulse that emboldened her more.

She lifted her head. She had so little time. And the desire sluicing through her was so very strong, so very hungry.

His lips twisted as he read the need in her eyes. 'Tell me,' he said.

'Take me, please,' she asked simply and wrapped her hand around his throbbing girth. 'I want all of you.'

He put his hands on her waist and lifted her

back onto the bed, finally coming to lie with her. She wriggled, relaxing against the mattress and lifting her arms to welcome him against her. He kissed her again—lush and deep and she was so excited.

He gently pushed her legs wider apart, teasing her again with his fingers. He lifted his head and their eyes met. He didn't ask if she was sure, if she was ready, he already knew. For a moment there was only agreement and pure anticipation between them.

He finally moved, aligning his hips with hers, his breath with hers, his heartbeat with hers. And as he set his lips to hers he met her intent with his in a slow, inexorable slide of possession that made her gasp deep. Instinctively she threw her arm around his neck, holding him near even as he hesitated.

'Jade?' he asked.

She saw the strain in his body as he tried to be gentle and go slow with her. But the pressure within, the drive for more, grew until it became undeniable.

'Kiss me.' She didn't wait for his answer. She kissed him, moving her hips against his, breathing hard as she embraced the pleasurable pressure-filled waves of his deepening possession.

Sensation soared as he buffeted against her and she began to understand, began to meet him back, stroke for stroke as she discovered how fantastic this felt, and how she too could drive this. With a smothered growl, he pushed his palms against the firm mattress beneath her and levered up, driving deeper in a surge of unfettered passion. She let her hands slide, gripping his forearms, feeling his muscles work beneath her, against her. She gazed up, awed at his power and strength as he fiercely pushed as hard as he could into her and enjoying the utterly exquisite ride. She couldn't form words, only sound as she gasped with astounded pleasure and he was the same. Grunting now with every pulse, every pound. And then he collapsed again, holding her more tightly than she'd ever been held, trapping her while at the same time imprisoned within her. She held him so fiercely. They were both shaking, almost violently convulsing as ecstasy overtook both mind and muscle.

Alvaro made himself gather the strength to lift away; he'd suffocate her if he stayed where he was. Her long drawn-out sigh in response almost brought him to his knees again. He'd tried to stay gentle, tried to take the time…but she'd come apart around him and he'd charged headlong into the fire with her like a man who'd lost it completely. But now she needed more again. He read it in her eyes and he heard it in her breathlessness.

'I like it when you hold me,' she whispered. 'I like it when you surround me so completely.'

Yeah, he liked that too. He liked the lock of her

arms around his back and her thigh hooking over his hip so he could surge deeper. He liked being so close to her that there was no getting closer, but trying anyway with bared skin and salty sweat and sweet pleasure. She'd arched and he'd thrust, over and over until he was drowning in the heated, silky prison of her body, until that pleasure hit, until there was nothing like this satisfied exhaustion in all the world.

Now her long hair was a tangled mess, knotting them together, and her face was flushed as she gazed up at him. Amazement gleamed from her pleasure-bruised eyes and he had never seen anyone as shockingly beautiful in his life.

'Alvaro.'

It was a whisper that ricocheted through to his soul. 'I know.'

She was tired, but she needed another kind of closeness. And for once, so did he.

'You feel so good,' he muttered as he rolled onto his back and pulled her limp form to rest over his.

'I'm so tired, but I want—'

'I know. We will. Soon,' he promised. Because so did he. 'It's not even nine o'clock, Jade.' He chuckled. 'We can take our time. We have all night.'

Only it didn't seem like long enough already.

CHAPTER SEVEN

JADE SLOWLY WOKE in a relaxed, comfortable heap, tangled in soft cotton sheets, soaking up the heated strength of the man curved behind her. It was her strangest, yet best ever way to wake.

They'd snatched only a couple of hours' sleep at most last night. After that first time, Alvaro had run her a bath and revived her with a fistful of cheap chocolate—all the commercial bars and wacky flavours that had been long banned from her diet by that zealous palace physician.

'No royal rules here,' he'd teased. 'And it's treat night, right?'

The whole night had been a decadent, delicious, pure lustful treat. Now, her pulse lifted, her aching body still seeking more.

'You must be used to getting breakfast in bed,' he murmured.

'I have a maid who brings me a coffee in the morning.'

'With cream and sugar, right? I'll get it.'

His warmth was gone before she had the chance to answer. She sat up. So it was over already?

For a panicked moment she couldn't believe what she'd done. What if there were cameras outside? What if she was caught somehow and everyone found out?

Would it matter?

Her father wasn't alive to judge or punish her. It wasn't an external threat troubling her. It was Alvaro himself. How did she face the man who'd touched her with such profound intimacy? It had felt beyond physical.

It's not.

She was feeling biochemistry—oxytocin, serotonin, dopamine. Her body's biology was encouraging her to stay and mate again. All animal instinct. And that adrenalin fix? The rush of the unknown and the unexpected?

That was everything Alvaro had treated her to last night.

But it was over, and she needed to get out of there. Her composure was suddenly shockingly precarious and she'd *never* lost her composure before this week. She'd never lost her virginity either. Until Alvaro.

Memories swept over her, invoking a real, raw response from her body. She shivered. She couldn't let him distract or delay her departure. Self-preservation insisted she end this now. If she stayed it would soon become a whole other day and a whole other night and that would become too intense. And impossible to walk away from. She couldn't let that happen. It wasn't what he wanted. Or what she wanted either.

She needed this time on her *own*. Wasn't *that* why she was here?

She quickly hunted about for her panties and pulled on her slip before finding her way from his bedroom back to the kitchen—desperately scooping her black dress up off the floor from where they'd left it last night.

He'd glanced up as she walked in and put down the cup he was holding. A glint kindled in his eyes as he watched her back away with the crumpled dress in hand. 'Not staying for coffee?'

Silently she shook her head. So awkwardly she darted back into the hallway and quickly pulled on her dress over her slip. She was desperate to escape.

'So what now?' he asked softly when she stepped back into the kitchen. 'You've no more work to worry about. You're free to do anything. What's your plan?'

She didn't really have one.

'Neon lights?' he prompted.

'Sure.' She'd focus on those external adventures. Seize on them as a means of avoiding the awkwardness rippling through her and that ache for intimacy welling inside. 'Ice skating at the Rockefeller centre. Eating doughnuts or a pastry outside Tiffany's or something, right? Times Square.' But her smile slipped, and she scrambled to think of more. 'Art galleries. All the exciting, fun things a tourist ought to do in New York in December.'

'Sounds like you have quite the list.'

'Yes.' She was determined to make the most of every one of *those* iconic experiences too. '*Christmas* in New York—it's my one and only chance.'

'But isn't Monrova all snow and sleighs and bells and warmly spiced Christmas baking?'

'In some homes, I'm sure it is.'

'But in the palace?'

'Just another day. Normal lessons continued. There was no extended family gathering. I had dinner with my father in the dining room as I did every night. And received the usual lectures.'

'But last night you told me you were spoilt.'

'I was. Just not especially at any of those kinds of things. So this year, this once, I want the full Christmas.'

He blinked. 'The full Christmas? What even is that?'

'I don't really know.' She began to smile. 'Like something from the movies?'

His jaw dropped. 'The movies?'

'Yeah, you know. All those good ones where people go the extra mile to find that one perfect present for their child, or they get through the snowstorm against all the odds to be with their loved ones...'

'It's not really like that, Jade.'

'No?' She glanced at him.

'Those movies make you think everyone is having the best time. They're not. I don't think *anyone* is.'

'No?' What had Christmas been like for him?

'Never. People set their expectations *way* too high. It's distant family stuck together for too long, drinking too much, and every time it gets so ugly...' He shuddered.

'You're cynical.'

He lifted his hands. 'It's how I see it.'

'You mean how it was for you?'

'You know I didn't have a normal family structure, so Christmas wasn't any of that for me, either.'

'You never had Christmas with family?' She was shocked. 'I'm sorry.'

'Not your fault, Jade.' He breathed out. 'Not mine either.'

But that throwaway comment weighed heavier than it should.

For the first time she didn't think he was being honest. Not with her, but with *himself*. And the tension within his muscular frame now? She shouldn't pry when she had no right. This was just physical. A one-night stand. She'd forgotten that fact so quickly. Yet she couldn't stifle her curiosity completely.

'So what did you do on Christmas Day? How do you know so much if you weren't with—?'

'I worked.'

'You what?'

'Christmas Day is an opportunity, Jade. There are *very* big tips to be got from large unhappy family parties. Ellen worked it every year, as did I, as soon as I was old enough.'

She stared at him. 'Do you still work on it?'

'Absolutely. It's a strategy day. I plan the year ahead.'

'Christmas is a *strategy* day?' She choked with an outrage that she didn't even need to exaggerate. 'That's even worse than *my* dreary day.'

He laughed. 'How is it worse? It's super productive. I like the peace and quiet. I achieve a lot.'

As she gaped at him she heard a familiar buzzing sound. It was Juno's phone. Startled, she whirled to hunt out her bag. But her phone stopped ringing before she could answer it. She glanced at the screen.

Jade.

Which meant *Juno* was trying to phone her— why?

Jade knew why. She'd seen it yesterday in a newspaper left on a table at a café she'd stopped at for lunch. Juno had been photographed with Leonardo at the Winter Ball in Monrova—and their shared glance wasn't one of two near-strangers being very proper and polite with each other. The way Leonardo had been looking at Juno? And then there were more photos of the two of them in Severene?

Jade knew Juno had wanted to talk to him. She'd been unusually concerned that Jade was considering a political union with him. She'd told Jade not to trust him. And yet—from those pictures? The media was salivating over an imminent engagement. Only problem was, they thought Juno was Jade.

'Everything okay?' Alvaro was watching her intently.

She grabbed Juno's leather jacket. 'I'd better get going. I need to return that call.'

'You could—'

'I need to go.' She was suddenly desperate to get away from him while she could. Thank heavens for Juno—she'd literally been saved by the bell of her phone.

'Sure.' He let her go.

But just as she reached the door he grabbed her arm.

'You're okay?' he asked.

She paused. That one touch was a reconnection that pushed aside her embarrassment to the joy still bubbling below.

'I'm so much better than okay,' she confessed. It had been amazing. 'I hope you are too.'

He stilled, his expression softened, his hold relaxed. And she took her chance to escape.

She quickly got out of the building into the crisp air. People were going about their daily business. It seemed as if nothing cataclysmic had happened in anyone else's world. Only hers.

She couldn't believe she'd slept with her sister's boss. No one could ever know. Ever. Not even Juno. It would make things weird for her at work and that was the last thing Jade wanted to happen. So she couldn't tell her sister. Not ever.

Drawing in a breath, she returned her sister's call.

'Juno, it's so good to hear your voice,' she whispered as she walked along the pavement, struggling to pull her thoughts together. 'Sorry I couldn't get to the phone straight away… It's… It's pretty early here.' And she was wearing the same clothes she'd been wearing last night. And she'd just left Juno's boss half dressed. And she'd *slept* with him. She drew in a deep breath of wintry morning air. 'I thought we agreed we wouldn't contact each other, just in case?'

'Jade… I… It's wonderful to hear your voice too.'

Jade stilled, hearing a tearful breathlessness in Juno's voice. Had something happened? She paused on the pavement, that press photo she'd glimpsed at the café yesterday popping back into her mind.

'I'm sorry I woke you up,' Juno added. 'And I know I'm not supposed to call, but...'

'Juno, what's wrong?'

'Something, something's happened, Jade. Something... I really did not expect...' Her sister's voice trailed off again.

Intuition rang loud in Jade's ears. 'Is this about Leonardo, and your state visit to Severene?' Jade tackled it directly. 'You make a great couple.'

'We're not a couple,' Juno answered so instantly that Jade had to smother a smile.

'Are you certain?' she queried gently. 'You look really happy together in all the press coverage. And by the way, you're doing a stunning job impersonating me. Better than I could do myself.' Juno looked more at ease with people than Jade ever felt.

'That's not true, Jade. I'm just good at faking it,' Juno said.

While Jade didn't know much about relationships, she didn't think that obvious chemistry with King Leo could be faked. 'You're not faking anything, Ju, you're a natural,' Jade said wistfully. And it wasn't just that sizzle, it was those smiles with those people who'd come to greet them in Severene. 'I always said Father was wrong not to consider you as his successor, and now I get to say I told you so.'

There was a moment of silence. 'Aren't you angry with me?' Juno asked.

'Why would I be angry?' Jade asked, amazed. She was delighted to see her sister in her rightful place.

'Because I'm not supposed to be in Severene? Because this swap was never supposed to get this complicated? Because I could end up completely screwing up Monrova's relationship with her neighbours.'

Jade thought for a moment, then answered calmly. 'No, I'm not angry about any of that.' Because it had got complicated for her too, so quickly. 'I've come to realise, seeing the press reports of you two, that Leonardo and I were never meant to be together. I'm really glad you persuaded me to come to New York.'

She'd realised she needed to slow down on that decision making. She was still young. She had time to think things through.

'It's been an eye-opening experience for me,' she added. 'I've discovered so much about myself and there's so much more to learn.'

There was so much she wished she could learn with Alvaro. But she'd had her one night and it hurt to remember it was over. So instead she focused on her sister. 'I also think it's super cute that there seems to be something developing between you two.'

'There's nothing developing between us. Nothing permanent anyway,' Juno murmured. 'It's just… There's a lot of chemistry between us and I like him more than I ever expected to.'

'Are you sure there's nothing more between you?' Jade asked softly. 'From the press reports I've seen, he looks at you in a way he's never looked at any of the other women he's dated.'

'No. There's nothing more,' Juno said, but she sounded unsure. 'Jade, I just… What I need to know, the reason I called, is… If Leo and I jump each other tonight. I mean, he's asked me and I… I really want to go for it. Because, you know, chemistry.' Juno drew in a breath.

Jump each other? Jade chuckled inside at her sister's choice of words. She guessed she'd 'jumped' Alvaro last night.

'We've agreed it won't mean anything beyond the physical. That it won't have any political implications. That the marriage is a whole separate issue.' Juno continued her rapid explanation. 'But if you'd rather we didn't… I mean, I don't want to mess things up for you… With Leo.'

'Juno, you're not serious—what possible claim would I have on Leonardo?' Jade almost laughed.

'Well, you know, you were considering marrying him a week ago.'

Jade did laugh then. A cold marriage of convenience now seemed appalling. Now she understood what the sacrifice would be if she were to marry solely for political reasons. She couldn't believe she'd actively been considering it—why on earth had she? And then she remembered. 'The marriage was always just about securing a trade relationship and uniting our two kingdoms.' Her ancient advisors had wanted it as a neat and tidy option. But it had been a way of avoiding personal uncertainty as well. 'I can't believe I ever thought that would be okay.'

'Jade, you don't sound like yourself.' Juno asked, 'Are you sure everything is going okay in New York?'

'It's… Yes, it's been really transformative in a lot of ways,' Jade said, trying not to let all her crazy thoughts explode out of her. 'I'm discovering things about myself I didn't realise. Not all of which I like.'

Her naivety. Her recklessness, tolerance, acceptance, her silence…and her *selfishness*.

'What things?' Juno asked. 'There's nothing about you not to like.'

'I used to think the same thing.' Jade laughed but she didn't feel it. She'd thought she'd been so good, so dutiful…whereas really? She was a coward.

'If something's happened, Jade, you can tell me, or we could swap back. Now.'

'No. I don't want to swap back, not yet,' she said swiftly. She didn't want to end it for Juno already. And she needed to straighten out her own head before she headed home. She *needed* this time. So much more than she'd realised. 'I'd really like to stay until New Year's Eve, like we agreed. Plus, I don't want you to miss your chance to jump Leo,' Jade added with a choked laugh. 'Unless you need to...'

'No, I don't want to swap back yet either...' Juno admitted.

'Listen, Ju, I've got to go.' Jade made herself get moving before she confessed everything to her sister. 'I've got a busy day ahead of me,' she fudged. It wasn't a complete lie; it would be a busy day recovering from the night of her life. 'But whatever you and Leonardo do, or don't do, you have my blessing. Okay?'

Her sister deserved some fun. Jade desperately wanted her to be happy.

'Okay.'

But Juno had said she and Leonardo had agreed it wouldn't be anything more than physical, that it was just chemistry, and now Jade knew that wasn't as easy as it sounded.

'But do me a favour,' she added swiftly before ending the call with Juno. 'Don't underestimate your feelings for him. They might be stronger than you think.'

Because that was the fear gnawing inside her— that the reason she'd told Alvaro she was 'so much better than okay' was that *it* had been so much *more* than physical. And now, the desire for more with him still tempted her to risk everything all over again.

But she was Queen and she *couldn't*. She could only be grateful that she'd had the night she had. Now, she needed to focus on *herself.* That was what Alvaro had shown her. She needed to speak up and strengthen her own damn spine.

Liberation swept over her. She and Juno had endangered themselves with this switch. But if she could time travel she'd choose to do the same again. No regrets. By the sound of things, Juno had none either. They could sort out any resulting mess once Jade was back home. But one thing was certain and it had been certain from first thing Monday morning. There was no way Jade was ever marrying King Leonardo or any other suitable prince her advisors recommended…

But she couldn't marry for love either. Her parents had tried and look how that had worked out. They'd fallen in love so quickly and out again only a few months later. They'd come from different worlds. And the mess it had made of their lives? Now, she knew there was nothing to be gained from a reckless, passionate relationship. Fortunately, the fact that she couldn't go ten seconds without thinking about Alvaro Byrne wasn't anything to do with love. It was lust. Simple, basic, bone-deep lust. And what had happened between them was perfect. Finite and perfect.

Honestly? She didn't think she'd ever marry *anyone*.

CHAPTER EIGHT

ALVARO PACED AROUND his apartment. She'd wanted immediate escape. She'd turned as soon as she could, trying to leave without drama, her face aflame in awkward embarrassment… But when he'd stopped her something else had emerged. Not the deeply ingrained politeness, not the ex-virginal embarrassment, but a pure, personal, simple admission.

She'd said she was 'so much better than okay' and then, *'I hope you are too.'*

That sweet wish for him had glued him in place—but he'd been unable to admit the same. Frankly he'd been unable to even breathe. Not before she'd already left.

She'd required no post-mortem. Apparently had no regrets either.

But that was good, wasn't it? He'd wanted—needed—her to go, too. He too wanted nothing, no last words, to spoil the perfection of their night together. And it would be spoilt eventually if they saw each other again.

He'd spoil it. Somehow.

He knew a moment in time was all they could ever have.

But he hated how empty his home suddenly felt. How desolate and vast his bed now was. He'd loved the curling length of her hair, the creaminess of her back, the narrowness of her waist and the flare of her hips…slender but sweet and soft. Irritated, he scratched the back of his neck and headed to the shower.

The next day he went out of town on a totally unnecessary field trip to sign the deal that had been under discussion for so long. It didn't matter that his own office was closed, he never stopped working. And the distance meant seeing her was impossible.

But that didn't stop him thinking about her. And in the end he couldn't resist phoning her.

'Alvaro? What's wrong?'

He winced. Did there have to be something wrong for him to phone? 'I'm checking up on your Christmas spirit. Have you been ice skating yet?'

'You should have seen me. I nailed it.' Her laughter was literally like bells.

Too much Christmas thinking. Too much missing…

'You've probably been skating since before you could walk.'

'I did find the rink a little small and crowded for my triple axel,' she joked.

He couldn't stand the thought of her ice skating on her own around that damned rink. 'And you saw the tree?'

'It was awesome, yes.'

'And how many lights?'

'Lots. Really good window displays too.'

Window displays? Wow. It all sounded ridiculously sad to him. 'What else?'

'Are you living vicariously through my Christmas experiences?' she teased. 'You don't even like Christmas.'

'I never said that,' he protested. 'I said I *work* Christmas.'

'You said Christmas was distant families getting drunk and miserable.'

'You've seen otherwise?'

'I've seen lots of family groups in restaurants. They look happy to me.'

'You only got a glimpse. You've got to see them at the end.'

'Well, I'm hardly going to stand around for hours outside, peering through the windows and watching them like some stalker.'

He grimaced at the image. Yeah, she was isolated. She shouldn't be doing those things alone. She should have family or friends with her to enjoy it with. But she had none. The only person who knew the truth of her life right now was him.

He returned to Manhattan two nights later. He stripped the bed. Even bought new linen—midnight blue, anything to make it different from how it had been when she'd been there with him. But he still couldn't sleep, couldn't stop seeing her smiling and her pretty form supine and the soft stretch of her creamy skin with the dew of sweat and the stain of colour in her face as he'd aroused her. So slow, so delicious, so worth every precious moment. The slippery sweetness of her taste. Being with her had been the hottest experience of his life and the ache of desire in his body now was enough to send a man insane.

But that wasn't what was really messing him around. It was his conscience. That sense of having done something wrong. But the mistake wasn't having had her, but in leaving her alone since.

That had been no ordinary night. And she faced no ordinary week. And he was flooded with something so much bigger than regret.

He woke early and went to the gym, desperate to burn off his frustration. It didn't work. That jaded, irritable feeling within only grew. He stalked to the coffee shop and got a triple shot. Waiting for it to be made, he glared out of the window, then his gaze dropped to the table beside him, and the paper spread on it. He flicked through a couple of pages, knowing what he'd find. Sure enough, there were more pictures of 'Queen Jade', aka Princess Juno, and King Leonardo, gallivanting around Severene, doing royal walkabouts and other feeding-the-media-frenzy things.

Jade had said there'd been some speculation about that stupid possible marriage—but these weren't whispers, these were screaming headlines and they sparked Alvaro's fury. Had Jade seen these pictures? What was her sister playing at? Was Jade seriously still contemplating some kind of political marriage? Was that why she'd been so keen to leave him so early the other morning? Was this all part of some crazy plan?

No. That wasn't Jade. She was too straight. And she'd been so determined to fix her job for her sister. So determined to be good. To not offend *anyone*. She was dutiful to the point of damaging her own future.

She'd said she wanted a few weeks of freedom. Some space to do the iconic Christmas things… Alvaro had never had the most abundant or joyful of Christmases, but he thought he'd actually had more than she had, even when he'd worked all day.

Fairy lights and fir trees…she'd had restrained decoration but never heartfelt detail. Not the closeness and comfort of family or even friends…those fun times that he too had seen in so many Christmas movies or season specials of nostalgic TV shows.

At the end of a long Christmas Day, he and Ellen had at least had each other. She'd tried her best to give him something even small. So now he gave her all he could in return.

If Jade wanted to experience some real Christmas joy, maybe he could help her. Maybe they could both do something a little better than their usual Christmases?

By Thursday he couldn't stand it a second longer. He couldn't stop thinking about those pictures of Juno with King Leonardo and his anger at Jade being all alone bubbled. What the hell were they all playing at? Jade's apparent docility regarding that so-called dutifulness infuriated him. Why did she have to sacrifice every element of her life for her crown and country? This wasn't the fifteen hundreds. People were allowed private lives. People were allowed some *fun*.

She was used to having an austere Christmas. So was he. And usually the thought wouldn't bother him at all. But the point of this time away was for her *not* to have that. She should have something more than aimlessly walking around city streets alone—even if it was Manhattan with all the bright lights it had to offer. He could do better than that. He wanted her to have more non-royal duty time. More fun. And for that she needed…if not family, then a friend.

After all, there was no reason why they couldn't be *friends*, was there?

His conscience told him exactly why.

Alvaro wasn't used to being a friend. Or having one. He was happy to be that loner who knew precisely what his value was to others—on the sports field back when he was a youth, as an entrepreneur, an investor, as a boss…and yes, as a lover. And if he didn't deliver, then he was no longer valued. And definitely not wanted.

The affairs he had never became anything more than a few weeks' fling. He gave into the lust, got it out of his system, moved on. It was only sex, after all. But that wasn't what he and Jade had done. Which was exactly why they couldn't do it again. She was more forbidden now than when he'd thought she was working for him. Not just because she was vulnerable. But because he was afraid he was too. But he couldn't resist phoning her once more.

'Alvaro?'

It wasn't right how happy he was to hear her carefully modulated tones again. Nor was it right how much he liked to make her breathless, to make her forget what it was she'd been going to say. Only right now *he* was the one who'd forgotten what words he'd meant to utter.

'Boss?' she teased.

And that was it. The moment he knew. He gripped the phone more closely and grabbed his car keys. 'Have you been on the eggnog already?'

He finally knocked on her door and then she was there. Slim jeans, thin sweater, wide, wide eyes. His body seized.

Don't kiss her. Don't kiss her. Don't kiss her.

'Alvaro?' She stood back from the doorway. 'What are you doing here?'

'Not kissing you,' he said brainlessly. Then he flinched and hustled to pull his head together. 'Just getting that out there first up,' he clarified more softly. 'I'm not here for that.'

'Okay.'

But that crestfallen hint in her eyes hit him like the thinnest, most deadly of blades. He could kick himself for his lack of tact. He couldn't admit how much he wanted to now. It would mess things up for her, wouldn't it? And that damn political marriage she was going to have to agree to some time in the next decade or so.

'I thought you'd be out already, doing all the things. It's after ten.'

'I'm just…' She drew a breath. 'Why are you here?'

'I don't want you to be alone for Christmas.'

'I'm quite used to being alone, Alvaro.' She went to close the door on him. 'It's not your concern.'

Her pride was back. Her politeness. Her refusal to express her emotions and her desires. *Queen Jade* herself.

'I'd like to show you some things.' His mouth felt as if it were stuffed with cotton wool. He was making such a mess of this.

She folded her arms across her chest. 'What things?'

'Just…things.' He realised this wasn't going as well as he'd thought it would. What had he expected? 'I mean—'

She was growing chillier by the second. 'I thought we weren't going to see each other again.'

'I think that was unnecessary caution on my part.'

'Caution?'

'I don't believe you'll fall in love with me just because we had sex and might spend a few days together.'

'Was *that* your concern?' Her jaw dropped and there was a glint in her eyes and he just knew she was thinking he was an arrogant jerk.

She was right. He had been.

'I don't wish to interfere in your life's plans,' he said.

She actually smiled but it was all queen. 'Nothing comes before my duty to my country.'

'I realise that now. I'm sorry. I was arrogant before.'

'Before? You're not any more?'

'It's possible I might relapse,' he said cautiously, watching for Jade to return.

'Would it be terrible for me to fall in love with you?' She studied him carefully.

'Yes. It could never work out.'

'It wouldn't work out with just me? Or with anyone?'

'Anyone,' he answered immediately and irritably. He had no idea how they'd got onto this. 'But especially not you.'

'Because of the Crown.' She actually nodded. 'I think it's best that we don't sleep together again. Definitely.'

'You do?'

'Once was a considered risk. A thrill, of course. But more than once wouldn't be rational. It would be reckless stupidity.'

Being with him again would be reckless *stupidity*? The stupid thing was that even though he'd decided there was no way they could be intimate again, now that she'd said the same thing he instantly wanted to fight back. And fight hard.

You always want what you can't have. And what would be so, so bad for you.

It was the human condition, wasn't it? That weakness, that failing…to be consumed by transient, addictive desires. That was the kind of thing that ruined people's lives. His didn't matter, but he wasn't ruining hers.

'Come on, you need to pack a bag.'

'You want me to leave with you now?'

'As I said, I don't want you to be alone for Christmas.'

'It's not Christmas.'

'It's close enough.' He offered her a grin. 'Don't

be a grinch. It's the holiday season. Go pack enough for a few days. We'll be back just after Christmas.'

'You're inviting me to spend all of Christmas with you?'

The temptation to lean close and kiss her almost overwhelmed him. He'd convince her quickly enough that way. But distracting them both with sex wasn't allowed. Not this time. They'd even agreed on that.

'Go pack your bag.'

'I get no choice? You're abducting me?'

And damn if she didn't look as if she liked that idea.

'I think of it as more of a rescue than an abduction. You want to stay home in a tiny apartment all by yourself for Christmas Day?'

Her expression flickered and he glimpsed the loneliness he'd recognised in her before.

'You wanted some other kind of Christmas, Jade. I can't promise everything, but it might be better than usual.' His lips quirked. 'It'll definitely be different. No palace. I promise.'

He watched her green eyes widen but she was silent. So silent, even when he could see the acquiescence, the *want* in those eyes. And he sighed.

'Abduction it is.'

CHAPTER NINE

IMPOSSIBLE MAN. Impossible to ignore. Impossible to resist.

Jade pulled an old carry-all down from the top of Juno's wardrobe. It was larger than her little flight bag and she quickly stuffed warm clothes into it, somehow stupidly afraid that if she didn't hurry, he might change his mind and leave without her.

Her heart skipped as she snatched up her toiletries bag and tossed it in as well. She'd been close to saying no, stupidly hurt by that barrier he'd instantly put between them when he'd arrived. But then her inner recklessness had whispered again. The same whisper that had seen her say yes to her sister's switch plan. She had so few days left, why shouldn't she enjoy them?

Honestly, she'd absorbed all the Christmas window displays she could stand and had breathed in the holiday mood as she'd passed restaurants and bars and convivial people celebrating. But night fell earlier and earlier and the crowds on the pavement with their hats and coats and bags of shopping had brushed by her as they'd scurried to be where they were needed or wanted. And it had left her too aware of those others like her, the ones on the edges. Alone.

She'd come back to Juno's apartment and filled the fridge with sugary snacks. All the things her father would have totally disapproved of. But the chocolate bars had reminded her too much of the midnight recovery snack she'd had with Alvaro Byrne.

And now he was back. But not for *that*. Yet she'd glimpsed fire in his gaze and guessed that he was battling temptation too. She wasn't the only one still feeling it. And suddenly that became part of the fun ahead—the challenge, the sparks that had flown between them from the first moment they'd met? It was exhilarating. Being around him made her feel *alive*.

Yes. He was impossible to deny.

Minutes later, he glanced at the green jacket she'd shrugged on over the top of her thin sweater and jeans, then reached forward and took the carry-all from her. He turned and led the way without a word.

'Not the sports car this time?' she asked as he remotely unlocked the large black sedan parked right outside.

He didn't reply.

'Where are we going?' She tried again once

they were both seated and belted and he'd already turned on the ignition.

'The coast.' He put the car in gear. 'But we're making a couple of stops along the way, okay?'

'You're the boss.'

He stiffened and she smothered her smile. Yes, he wasn't as unaffected as he liked to make out.

Alvaro wasn't slow in getting them out of town. Jade stared resolutely ahead, defying her inner desire to simply stare at him. In the black turtleneck jumper and dark blue jeans he looked all moody muscle and appallingly mesmerising.

Companionship for Christmas. That was all he was offering. *Not* kisses.

That arrogance of his annoyed her intensely, but as he drove she slowly relaxed and a bubble of pleasure broadened inside. She was glad to get out of town and see something—*anything*—new. The changing landscape was the perfect distraction.

'We're heading to New Haven,' he suddenly said in a clipped voice. 'We'll stay there the night. We need to visit someone tomorrow morning and in the afternoon we'll head to my place.'

Her curiosity roared. 'Who's the friend?'

His hands tightened on the steering wheel. 'Ellen.'

Jade remembered, she was the one whose photo he had, the one he'd said saved him. She glanced at the tension in his hands. 'You grew up in New Haven?'

He shook his head. 'That's where she lives now. And she's still working Christmas, she takes in all the waifs and strays she encounters, so she's providing lunch for a random bunch of people.'

She picked up on the frustration. 'You don't approve?'

'Of course, I do.' He sighed. 'But she does too much. She's older now and she doesn't have to…'

'How many people come to her lunch?'

'Half a dozen maybe? I never know the exact numbers. She cooks up a storm and serves the leftovers to the ones who drop in for days after.'

'She sounds amazing.' Jade smiled. 'People want to be around her?'

'Yeah,' he muttered. 'I guess they do.' He suddenly turned off the main road and wove in and around a few streets before pulling into a car park.

Jade stared out of the window. He'd stopped in the centre of a coastal village at the town green. It was festooned with gorgeous fairy lights and a small Christmas market with green and red bunting on the very pretty stalls. It looked delightful.

'Are we there already?' She followed his lead and got out of the car.

'No, but I feel like you need food,' he said shortly.

She laughed. 'I feel like you're projecting.'

'Probably.' He rubbed his hand across his stomach as he leaned to the side to stretch out the kinks in his back. 'Come on, they have the best pastries here.'

Jade focused on the small market ahead, refusing to wish it were *her* hand skimming over the washboard abs she knew were beneath the soft wool. Alvaro headed like a sweet-seeking missile, straight towards one stall, and she heard him order coffee and pastries.

'You've got to try one.' He held out the cardboard tray to her two minutes later.

She picked up one of the spheres of fried dough; it was drenched in honey and sprinkles. Sticky, sweet, so hot and one was simply never going to be enough.

He grinned as he watched her chew. 'Good, am I right?'

'So much better than good.' She sighed.

As they walked around the market, the warmth inside Jade wasn't from the small sweet pastries or the smell of Christmas spices, it was the company, the easing of the tension between them. Alvaro was clearly familiar with the market and the goods available—or at least the edible ones.

'You call in here every year?' she asked when he made a beeline for another stall—fudge this time, in an assortment of mouth-watering flavours.

'Absolutely.'

She liked that he had his own little Christmas tradition, even if he insisted on working the actual day. They took their time weaving along the stalls, admiring the decorations and hand-crafted garments for sale. She lost him briefly, when she paused by one trestle table, taken by an incredible display of miniature treats—gingerbread houses, Bundts and Christmas puddings.

'Are they edible?' she asked the woman behind the stall in amazement. They were so *tiny*.

'Of course.' She smiled. 'You're welcome to try a sample.'

'Thank you.' Jade beamed. Back home she'd never be allowed to eat market food without it being tested first. She'd only ever been offered pre-selected, triple-checked tastes. Here she could try anything she wanted to. And she did.

'They're so perfect, they must have taken so long to make,' Jade marvelled.

Those very particular edible presentations on tour were always fine and fancy, but the intricate piping on these tiny structures utterly amazed her.

'Could we take some of the houses to Ellen?' She turned to Alvaro when he walked back to where she'd lingered. 'For her Christmas dinner?'

'Sure, that'd be nice.'

The stallholder delightedly boxed up a dozen. Ten minutes later Alvaro carefully stowed them in the trunk of the car and then slammed it shut.

'Which did you prefer, by the way?' he turned to her to ask. 'The sweet dough balls or the fudge?'

'They were both delicious,' Jade answered.

Laughter lit his eyes and he shook his head. 'No. You can have only one. You have to choose.'

'Why do I have to choose?' She smiled. 'They were both amazing.'

His eyebrows lifted. 'Why is it so hard to pick a favourite? You must have an opinion on them.'

'Well, I don't.' She shrugged.

'Don't or *won't*?' The gleam in his eye was sharper now, not as amused. 'You're allowed your *own* opinion, Jade.'

'I am.' She nodded. 'But I'm also aware that I can't share it much.'

'Pardon?'

'Look,' she huffed. 'I know this might sound arrogant, but I have influence. And with that comes responsibility. I can't be seen to endorse one product over another. So I don't choose. I never choose.'

Alvaro theatrically glanced up and then down the path. 'Jade, I'm not sure if you've realised, but we're currently *alone*. No one is paying any attention to us. There are no cameras, and no one around for you to influence, other than me. And I won't be overly swayed by your opinion, I'm confident in my own tastes and desires.'

Her lips twisted. 'I'm aware of that.'

Truthfully, she was still getting used to the fact that there were no cameras on her when she went out. It wasn't normal not to have them. It had been drilled into her all her life—that any moment could and probably *would* be caught on camera. Remembering that horrible fact stopped her from doing things she shouldn't. Like challenging him to kiss her right now.

'You truly won't say which you prefer?' he asked.

'It's how I've been trained.'

His eyebrows shot up. 'So do you say you just like everything?'

'I can find something *positive* in everything,' she replied.

'Wow. So even if you hate something, you'll find something about it to bestow your approval on?'

She glared at him as her annoyance grew. 'You make it sound as if that's a bad thing.'

'It is. It's dishonest.'

'No, it's not. It's just…judicious. It's being kind.'

'Kind?' he scoffed. 'It's cowardly. You have to be able to admit when you don't like something. You have to have that freedom. That choice. Otherwise you just end up…bland. And in the end no one can trust a word that emerges from your mouth.'

She was suddenly hurt. 'I don't lie.'

He straightened up from the car and stepped closer. 'But you don't fully express yourself either.'

Horrible, hot resentment built within her at his judgment. Because she had with *him*. She had been so honest, so vulnerable, so exposed. And he knew it.

'I dare you to say what you like.' He stood right in front of her, his whisky-amber eyes hot and hard as if he were even angrier than she. Impossible.

'Tell me what you like,' he said. 'Tell me *one* thing you absolutely love and can't get enough of. That you'd do every day if you could.'

There was fire in her hurt and fury now. But she wasn't being provoked into saying something she *knew* he wanted her to admit.

'What do you want, Jade?' he pushed. 'Tell me one thing you really want.' Passion now burned in his eyes as well. 'You're allowed to say. You don't need my or anyone else's permission. Why is it so hard? You did with me once already.'

'That was different,' she muttered through clenched teeth.

'How?'

'Because it *was* once. Once. One night.' She didn't want to say it again. She didn't want to let him have that victory. But then it wouldn't be only his win, would it? It would be *hers* too.

So she stepped closer, unable to ignore the craving any more. 'I want you to be quiet,' she whispered furiously. 'I want you to stop goading me and start doing something else instead.'

'Something else?' He towered over her but still didn't touch her.

'You know already,' she growled at him. 'You want it too. You're as dishonest about that as I am. You didn't come back to kiss me? That was *such* a lie, Alvaro.'

'But *you* agreed it wouldn't be wise.'

'And it wouldn't.' She nodded, never more sure of that than she was right now.

This entire trip wasn't wise. Because she was so tempted by him and it was utterly impossible. Getting close to him again? Exploring that magic with him again?

She couldn't. Because it *hadn't* been 'just sex' for her. He'd made her want so much more.

'I'm supposed to be considering marriage to another man,' she said, reminding herself more than telling him.

Never mind that it was no longer the truth, it was a viable reason to make herself *step back*.

But the look in Alvaro's eyes flared and he stepped forward. 'Was that ever a serious consideration? And now? After...' He frowned as she coolly met his gaze. 'Wow. Is it seriously still on the cards for you?'

She suppressed a shiver and stood her ground. If there was one way to put their chemistry on ice, this was it.

'I haven't ruled it out. But I need to see what he wants,' she fudged, regretting bringing the subject up.

'What *he* wants? So if he wanted to proceed, you would?'

'It's my duty—'

She broke off as he made a sound in the back of his throat.

'It is my duty,' she repeated, 'to do what is best for my country. Nothing and no one can come before my duty to the Crown.'

'You really believe that?' he softly, lethally questioned, leaning far, far too close. 'You really think that what *you* want comes second? That you have to sacrifice your life because of some duty you think you owe just because of some stupid birth order?'

She glared up at him, because she did believe exactly that.

'You're using it to hide,' he savaged her. 'Because you're too scared to stand up for yourself and for what you really want.' He drew in a jagged breath. 'I get that your father was strict, but you don't have to do as he says any more. You don't have to do as *anyone* says. You can be your own woman.'

'I'm the Queen of Monrova, Alvaro,' she said bloodlessly. 'I can *never* be my own woman.'

He pulled a torn piece of paper from his back pocket and shoved it into her hands. Jade stared at him a few seconds longer before dropping her gaze to unfold what he'd wanted to show her. It was torn from a newspaper—a spread of photos that she barely glanced at before holding it back out to him. 'I've already seen photos of Juno and Leonardo.'

'When?'

'The other day.' She'd seen those ones from the Winter Ball where they'd been dancing.

'Before we were together?' Alvaro's gaze drilled into her.

She hesitated and looked down again, smoothing out the paper he'd not taken back. 'It was after I'd asked you.'

'But did this impact on that decision?' he probed.

She shook her head. 'I did what I wanted.'

But now she stilled as she scanned the other pictures of Juno and Leonardo in this paper. Her sister looked *happy*. They were on a walkabout and Juno was bent, talking to a small child. She looked more relaxed than Jade ever felt on such an engagement and the obvious chemistry between them had columnists frothing at the mouth. And it certainly wasn't based on nothing. A wave of tenderness swept through Jade.

'Does he know?' Alvaro asked.

Jade couldn't bear to think about that. The press and the rest of the world thought that was her— *Jade*—with Leonardo. That this was the beginning of a great romance and the world was now anticipating a royal wedding to end all royal weddings. It would be an absolute fairy tale. It certainly would be fiction. How could they possibly continue with this when she returned to Monrova and they switched back? They wouldn't, of course.

'He knows she's Juno, right?' he asked again.

Surely Leonardo did. Jade trusted Juno; she was sure this would work out. Juno had been vehemently anti Jade's possible marriage of convenience with Leonardo. There were obviously feelings there that Jade hadn't been aware of. Maybe Juno hadn't been fully aware of them either.

But Jade could feel Alvaro watching her now. 'Stop trying to analyse me.'

'I'm trying to figure out what you're feeling.'

'What I'm *feeling* doesn't matter.' That wasn't relevant to her role as Queen.

'It matters to me.'

The soft anger with which he said that broke something inside her apart. 'Stop feeling sorry for me.'

'Why shouldn't I?' That anger in his voice built. 'I thought you just said you were still considering marrying this guy. Aren't you hurt by this?'

'Of course not,' she argued. 'I'm many things, but I'm not hurt.'

'Then *tell* me the many things. Tell me even *one* of them.'

'I want Juno to be happy,' she snapped. 'She *deserves* to be happy.' And she hoped more than anything that she was reading Leonardo's expression right.

Alvaro nodded. 'And you don't deserve that?'

'It doesn't need to be a comparison all the time.' Jade shook her head. 'Just because we're twins.' She hated that and knew Juno did too. 'It's okay for me to consider her without thinking of myself the next second. I want *her* to be happy.'

'Okay.' Alvaro paused. 'But I'm interested how this impacts on you. On what you want for yourself.'

She closed her eyes briefly. 'I want to do what's best and what's right for Monrova.'

'And what's that?' he kept pushing her. 'As if who you marry is going to matter?'

'It's *not* going to matter,' she exploded at him. 'Because I'm not marrying *anyone*.'

'*Finally.*' His stance eased and his anger ebbed. 'You've finally seen the light. Now let's get going before it gets too dark and cold.'

But Jade's anger hadn't fallen—suddenly she was furious with him. For a few days there she'd been fine about abandoning any arranged marriage plan. But now? Now it felt as if he'd left her with nothing. He'd made her face how alone she really was. And how was she ever to meet someone? Who would ever want to join her in the extraordinarily proscribed life she led? Not him, that was for sure.

A silent hour's drive later Alvaro pulled up outside a hotel. The receptionist's eyes widened when they walked in and Jade knew the woman had recognised her——hopefully as Juno, not Jade, so she remained quiet when Alvaro signed them both in.

'She recognised you,' Alvaro murmured as he declined a porter and carried their bags himself. 'Which is why this is your room here, while mine's a few along.' He paused at the door and passed her bag to her.

'That's the only reason we have separate rooms? For the look of it?' she asked as lightly as she could through gritted teeth. 'I thought you didn't bring me along to kiss me.'

His gaze intensified, drilling through her. 'I think we ought to eat out. I'll knock on your door in half an hour.'

Food? Again?

She half groaned, half laughed, and let herself into her room. Maybe eating was the perfect displacement activity for them both.

She tossed Juno's carry-all onto the bed and unzipped it to find a fresh sweater to wear. But given she'd packed in a hurry, she ended up tipping the entire jumbled contents onto the bed. As she went to lift the empty bag away, she felt a hard object in the interior pocket. She frowned, not remembering what it was she'd put in there. She unzipped it and paused when she saw the sheaf of papers. She *hadn't* put this in there.

Her blood chilled as she realised these documents must be Juno's. Jade had thought the bag was empty. But curiosity had her in its claws, because she'd caught a glimpse of photos in there, and she'd recognised the name on the top corner of one of the papers.

Alice Monroe.

Jade pulled out the pile before she could guilt herself into stopping. Because this was personal and private and she shouldn't…but why shouldn't she, when this was her mother, and her sister?

It was the photograph that consumed her first. Juno must've been about fifteen and she was standing. The defiant tilt to her mouth contrasted sharply with the sadness dulling her eyes. Jade recognised strain and pain and a world of things she shouldn't have had to face. Not alone. Not cast out.

Because the thin, worn woman she was standing next to at a slight distance? Their mother— Alice. That formerly beautiful, once celebrated actress. In this wretched instant-print snap, she was holding a glass at an angle and her addiction on her face. All the vitality she'd once had, sucked out of her.

But she'd known so little about her mother and of the world that Juno had grown up in. And seeing this discharge form now? From a city hospital where her mother had been briefly admitted to 'rehydrate'?

Jade had grown up in an abnormally strict

world, but Juno's simply hadn't been safe. She'd been alone and dealing with adult things from such an early age. Because there it was—her sister's handwriting, filling in the utilities forms when the banks were foreclosing. These few pieces of paper revealed so much.

Jade almost snatched up her phone. But she and Juno had vowed not to make contact unless there was a crisis. And this could hardly be called a crisis.

But her heart ached for her sister. For everything they'd missed out on together. They'd not been able to support each other the way they should have.

She thought about Juno's reasons for wanting these weeks in Monrova—they'd been layered. Juno had looked after their mother. And now she'd wanted to look after Jade regarding that marriage of convenience. But she'd not told Jade these details from her life here. She'd not confided in her.

Jade had been protected for so long. Jade, whom Juno still wanted to protect—from the big bad wolf she'd seen King Leonardo as.

As if Jade couldn't make decisions for herself?

And she'd not. She'd done everything her father had told her to. She'd only been considering that stupid marriage contract because of her father.

Why? Because she'd been too scared not to. Because she'd always been too scared.

No one seemed to think she could manage on

her own. That she could handle these decisions. They all wanted to guide her, to protect her. To have her as Queen, yes. But only ever a dutiful one. Because she'd not been vocal enough. She'd not *said* what *she* wanted.

Not the way Alvaro had encouraged her to. Not in any aspect of her life. Except the most intimate now. He wanted nothing more than for her to scream her desire. He wanted to please her, but not in the same way as so many others in her life wanted to please her. Not as Queen and servant, or Queen and subject, or as Queen and someone simply curious. But as equals.

He'd dared her to be open and honest about the littlest of things and she'd struggled with that. She'd spent her life being careful not to upset anyone—trained to be the ultimate diplomat.

Or was that *doormat*?

A low anger throbbed within her.

She loved that her sister wanted to care for her, but she didn't need her to. She didn't want Juno to feel that she had to protect her. *That* was the problem—that there was this assumption that Jade was somehow rarefied…more fragile, or more precious than other people?

Of course, she wasn't.

She'd been a coward. She should have stood up to her father years ago when he'd been awful to Juno, awful to her mother, awful to her. She should have challenged his old advisors. If she'd only had courage. Regret swamped her. The horrendous feeling of failure submerged her in acid. She presented this facade of capability, of being a perfectly studied monarch, when she was so far from it. When she was a far less than perfect person.

She'd not been *naive* in her consideration of a political alliance. She'd known what it would have meant and only a couple of weeks ago she'd been willing to accept discretion—to turn a blind eye while having no lover for herself. But what she'd said to Alvaro this afternoon was her truth now. She didn't want to marry. She *couldn't*.

That you could fall in love quickly? That was possible. She was horribly sure of it. It was about the only thing she was sure of right now.

The knock on her door startled her. Alvaro. She couldn't face his all-seeing eyes like this. She couldn't hide the truth of her heart.

But he knocked again. 'Jade?'

She could hear his concern. She couldn't ignore him—he'd have security up here in a heartbeat.

'One second,' she called out as she got up and went to the door. She opened it a fraction. 'I'm sorry—'

His gaze narrowed instantly. 'What's wrong?'

He'd pushed her door wider and stepped into the room before she had the chance to answer. His gaze hit the scattered papers on the floor—

and that awful photo of her formerly glamorous mother and her strained-looking sister.

Jade knelt to gather the papers, but her hands were shaking. He was beside her in less than a second, helping her—emotionlessly, so politely not even looking. But she knew he couldn't avoid seeing it.

'The carry-all is an old bag of Juno's. I didn't realise it had anything in it,' she explained quietly without looking at him.

She put them back into the bag. She'd explain to Juno that she'd borrowed the bag, and she'd seen the hidden contents by accident.

'I once looked it up on the Internet,' she muttered on. 'My parents' romance was all so well documented. She was a famous actress, he was a handsome king...you know, the stuff of fairy tales.'

But not long after their marriage her mother had grown miserable, unable to cope with royal life in Monrova. And then, after the split, when sent away with one of her daughters, she'd been unable to cope with her 'freedom' back in the States.

Suddenly, to Jade, a life swamped in duty seemed safer after all.

'I had no idea how bad it was for Juno with our mother,' she said. 'I wish she'd told me.'

'Could you have done anything if she had?'

She shrugged. 'I don't know...but I didn't even get the chance. She should have confided in me,' she said sadly, leaning back in a heap against the end of the bed. 'She shouldn't have had to deal with all that on her own.'

'You dealt with things on your own too.'

'Not the same, Alvaro.' She shook her head. 'So not the same.'

'You can't beat yourself up for not knowing what she was dealing with. You were on the other side of the world, you had limited contact and you were barely an adult yourself. You didn't have much power to help either of them, Jade.'

'I could have been a support to Juno,' she whispered. 'But she didn't want that.'

He was silent a while. 'She probably wanted to protect you.'

'I don't *need* protection.' She hated the thought of people thinking she couldn't cope or that she wasn't wise enough to make her own decisions. Or didn't have something to give other people besides a smile and a polite wave. 'She didn't need to do that for me.'

'You want to protect her too,' he pointed out with a wry smile. 'That works both ways, Jade. She feels that you have burdens of your own that she'd wished she could ease for you...the Crown, for one thing.'

She shook her head again. 'I had it easy compared to her.'

'Did you?' He sat next to her on the floor, his leg running the length of hers. 'You were left with an unloving father who didn't bother to get you anything for Christmas. Let alone anything more meaningful. You were probably terrified that if you messed something up, he'd boot you out too.'

She stared at the floor, her eyes stinging with tears. Because it had been exactly that. She'd been terrified of stuffing up. Of him yelling at her the way she'd heard him yell at Juno. Of being banished the way her mother had.

She'd worked so hard in every way to do and be all that he wanted. And he still hadn't noticed, hadn't softened...hadn't cared.

'Jade?' Alvaro cupped her face with his hand in that careful, tender way and turned her to look at him.

She couldn't speak, couldn't push past that lump in her throat as she gazed into the warmth of his eyes.

'Is that how it was?' he asked.

She was so stiff with agony, she could barely nod.

'I'm sorry,' he muttered.

'I...' She breathed in a hard breath. 'I just wish she'd talked to me.'

'It can be the hardest thing to say something painful...' he said softly. 'Even to someone...'

She nodded again. She knew.

That was how it was for him, wasn't it? Impossible to say something personal, even to a friend.

The silence between them grew as she gazed

into his beautiful, beautiful eyes and wished for other things to be different too.

'Jade...' His voice was strained. 'We really need to get out of this room.' He lifted his hand and ran his fingers through his hair.

She glanced up at him and attempted a feeble joke. 'You want to go to the gym?'

His face lit up at the thought she truly hadn't meant for real. 'Now that is an *excellent* idea.'

'I wasn't serious.' She really, *really* wasn't serious.

But he was already on his feet. 'There's one on level three.'

'You know that? Oh, my...of course you know that.'

'Come on.' He extended his hand to her and, heaven help her, she took it.

'I thought you wanted food,' she groaned.

'We can get something after. There's a Christmas carnival down the street. They have flashing lights, I promise.' He opened the door and went out into the corridor. 'I don't know about you, but I need to burn some energy.'

Five minutes later Jade found herself facing Alvaro, who'd already whipped off his sweater to reveal a tee that hugged that masculine vee of his body. Too well did she remember the heated wall of muscle that was his chest.

He danced in front of the boxing bag and winked at her. 'Spar with me.'

'You cannot be serious.' She lifted her hands in surrender instead. 'You're way bigger than I am.'

'I'll keep one hand behind my back.'

'And hop on one foot?' She shook her head and walked over to the equipment rack, leaving him to it. 'Not going to happen.'

But he was trying to make her laugh and it was working.

'There are things I could do with that skipping rope, Jade, if you don't want to use it in the usual way.'

She shot him a look and his laugh was low and sexy and then he turned and took a couple of playful swipes at the bag. She stared at his pure graceful strength and athleticism.

'You're not being fair,' she softly complained.

All the emotions he'd made her feel in the last twenty minutes?

'And you are?' he countered quietly. 'Look at you...just...'

'Just what?'

'Standing there.'

Warmth flooded her. He made her feel so wanted—at least in this one way.

'We both agreed the rules,' she breathed. 'We both understood them.'

'But you've broken other rules already this week, Jade. If you've done it once you can do it again.'

'Or perhaps I've learned my lesson.' She

stepped back. 'And all I've eaten today are some pastries. Let's go get something more substantial, shall we?'

'Oh, fine,' he growled.

Two hours later they walked back to the hotel. Jade hadn't laughed as much in years. Alvaro had unleashed his ultra-competitive side and she'd been unable to resist the challenge. With his apparently bottomless supply of quarters, they'd thrown darts at balloons for far too long before eating unidentifiable meat on a stick and piping-hot fries. She'd refused the neon cotton candy because she didn't need the sugar high to make her heart pound faster.

They'd talked of nothing serious. Nothing of her past or her future, only whether or not they should do the rifle range first or the big six. She'd loved watching his enthusiasm emerge. He had a dynamism like no one she'd ever met. Not recklessness—he was incredibly disciplined and energetic regarding his work, but he had a controlled zest that, once released, was infectious. And killer competitive spirit. In the final tally he won the most—offering her the obligatory oversized ugly plush toy alligator that secretly Jade was sure the operator gave him only because he'd spent so much money on the damn games.

'Not going to fit in my cabin baggage, sorry,' she'd demurred.

He'd laughed and given it to a family passing by.

And now, back in the hotel, he paused by her door.

'Let me know if you need anything,' he muttered.

And who was being unfair again now?

She stared up at him and that ripple of desire—of promise—made her shiver again. But she'd deny it still—not even say it to herself. 'I think I can manage everything fine on my own, thanks.'

Amusement and appreciation flared in his eyes. 'Maybe there'll come a moment when you can't,' he whispered, teasing retribution. 'Watch out then, Jade.'

And she couldn't resist responding, 'Is that a threat?'

He opened her door for her only to then step away. 'More of a promise.'

He'd meant it only as a joke, another little lightening of the atmosphere after her earlier emotion. But for her, it was all warning.

CHAPTER TEN

'IT WON'T TAKE LONG, but I need to check on her.'

'Of course.' Jade didn't mind how long it took, she was fascinated to be meeting someone who'd had such an impact on him.

But Alvaro had been quiet on the drive and now they'd pulled up outside a suburban house, his tension was even more palpable as he checked his phone with a frown.

Jade hadn't bothered even turning her phone on. The morning was too gorgeous and she was too intrigued. Now, as they got out of the car, she scooped up the box of tiny gingerbread houses and carried them up the path. Alvaro had no other gifts with him, which surprised her a little. But he'd just lifted his hand to knock on the door when it opened and an older woman stepped out. She gazed up at him for a moment then nodded. 'Alvaro.'

'Ellen.'

It was the briefest hug before the woman turned to scrutinise Jade with sharp interest. 'Have you brought a friend with you?'

Her audible amazement sent warmth flooding through Jade. She felt outrageously pleased that a woman with Alvaro was an obvious rarity.

'Ellen, this is—' Alvaro shot Jade a quick query.

'PJ,' Jade swiftly stepped in.

But she didn't want to lie to this woman. She'd discovered how much she *hated* lying. 'It's a pleasure to meet you, Ellen.'

Warmth—and avid curiosity—swirled from the slightly stooped figure. Ellen was older than Jade had expected, but she guessed the lines on her face were hewn not just from hard work, but from smiles too. Because it also took only a split second for Jade to see that Ellen absolutely adored Alvaro.

Of course, she did.

'Come in.' The elder woman hustled them. 'It's too cold to loiter out here.'

Jade glanced at Alvaro's bent head and saw the crooked smile he gave Ellen even though she'd already turned to lead them into her lounge.

Inside Jade didn't know where to look first. There were shelves stacked with books and board games—not ancient battered editions, but new ones covering every genre, and a wide variety of non-fiction. There were puzzles too. The place had a literal warmth to it, with a cosy fire heating the large room and thick coverings on the floor.

She caught Alvaro's eye and saw his quick wink, heard his low murmur. 'And the décor says…?'

That Ellen liked to welcome a wide range of people to her home. Jade had expected to like her—this was the woman who'd somehow 'saved' Alvaro—but seeing this, meeting her? She liked her all the more.

Jade held out the box of pastries to her. 'We've brought a few—'

'Alvaro,' Ellen turned and scolded him. 'You know that's not necessary. You've given me far too much already.'

'Don't look at me.' Alvaro spread his hands in mock innocence. 'These are from PJ.'

Ellen swivelled towards Jade. 'You'll forgive me, but finding places to put all the things he's sent me is impossible.'

This was clearly a source of ongoing banter between them, but Jade could play along.

'These are miniature cakes, Ellen,' Jade answered gently. 'They are *most* necessary.'

Ellen stared at her for a second, then laughed. 'Alvaro, you've found an ally.'

He just grinned. 'What do you need me to do, Ellen?'

'You couldn't just sit down and talk to me?'

'No.' He'd already pushed up his sleeves. 'Is that firewood delivery properly stacked?'

'Oh.' Ellen laughed again. 'Go on, then, I know you have to see it with your own eyes.'

He glanced at Jade. 'Want to come see—?'

'Of course, she doesn't,' Ellen swiftly answered before Jade could. 'We'll find a place to put these pastries.'

'I didn't bring her here to be subjected to an inquisition, Ellen.' Alvaro looked to Jade. 'You don't have to answer any questions, there's no penalty, just so you know.'

Jade felt absurdly shy but followed Ellen through to a large kitchen. She met people all the time in the course of her duties, but this sharp-eyed woman was important to Alvaro, even if he was reticent to admit how much. And that made her nervous.

'You've known Alvaro long?' Ellen asked.

'I met him through work,' Jade replied, smiling as the inquisition instantly began. 'He's been a good friend to me.'

Ellen's gaze sharpened. 'Has he?'

Jade maintained her smile and went for immediate diversion. 'Where would you like me to put these? I don't think they need refrigerating or anything, so I could just tuck them on that shelf over there?'

There was the smallest space because the shelves, like those in Alvaro's own kitchen, were incredibly well stocked.

'You see what I mean?' Ellen laughed.

'The wood store looks good.' Alvaro reappeared sooner than Jade expected.

'They're good lads.' Ellen nodded. 'They did it in record time.'

Alvaro washed his hands before checking the contents of the pantry and giving a satisfied nod. 'I'll get under way.'

'He comes every year to help with the preparations.' Ellen sighed to Jade, but pride was evident in her voice. 'He makes the Christmas butter.'

'The Christmas butter?' Jade laughed as she glanced across the table at him. 'Alvaro?'

He shrugged as he reached for an apron. 'It's the best and, no, I won't share the recipe. I have my own secret blend of nuts and spices.'

'It is the best.' Ellen nodded. 'I'll give him that.'

Of course, it was. Because Alvaro was the world's most competitive person in everything he attempted.

'It doesn't take long,' he said gruffly.

But Jade didn't want Ellen thinking she was making him cut this visit short.

'Can I help? Please let me help.' She rubbed her hands together nervously. 'Anything that doesn't require skill, that is.'

'You don't cook, PJ?' Ellen asked.

'Not really,' Jade mumbled apologetically.

'I'm sure you do other things,' the older woman said with that oddly brisk kindness. 'Not everyone can excel at everything, like that overachiever there.' She gave Alvaro a warm glare.

Alvaro had been looking thoughtfully at Jade.

'We can make a start on the potatoes for you, Nel. I know you hate peeling.'

'What I hate is the arthritis I get when I try.' Ellen grimaced. 'So, yes, thank you. You ordered far too many, even for us.'

Jade watched Alvaro gather equipment.

'I'll peel, you chop, okay?' he said.

'Sure.' She was just relieved she didn't have to stand there uselessly any more.

An hour passed swiftly as they slipped into a natural rhythm. Jade listened to the banter between Ellen and Alvaro—each ridiculously quizzing the other. Alvaro visibly relaxed and teased more. Once the potato mountain was peeled, he moved on to his famous butter—chopping a massive pile of nuts and dried fruit.

'Will you stay for lunch?' Ellen asked.

'You know we can't stay this time,' he said instantly.

'This time?' Ellen rolled her eyes and gruffly scolded him again. 'You flit in and tear up the place getting everything done and the second it is, you're gone. You never stay.'

'And you know there's always the next job to be done…'

'It's supposed to be a holiday,' Ellen grumbled before she turned to Jade. 'Come and admire my Christmas tree, PJ,' she ordered. 'So chef here can maintain the secrecy of his recipe.'

'It won't be long,' Alvaro reminded them as Jade dutifully followed Ellen to the dining room.

The tree was in one corner, but the room's real draw were the two large rectangular tables. Set end to end, they took up almost the entire space. An assortment of chairs was stacked in the corner while heaped on the end of the nearest table were packets of table decorations, Christmas-themed plates and tinsel. The courier sticker was still on the packaging of one and the name on it caught Jade's eye—Ellen Byrne.

Jade stilled, surprised. Alvaro had taken Ellen's surname? So for how long had they been in each other's lives? When had they met? And in what way had Ellen *saved* him? It was obvious they were close, and yet…

'You do this every year?' Jade sought to relieve some of her less intrusive curiosity.

'Yes, and Alvaro arrives every Eve to help.' Ellen straightened. 'It's not enough that he *pays* for everything.' Her expression tightened. 'He's always paying…'

'You don't like him to?' Jade asked.

'I wish he didn't feel that he has to,' Ellen muttered. 'And so much. Look at that pile of decorations. What am I supposed to do with them all?'

Jade chuckled. 'People like being able to do things for those they love. I guess this is something he can do?'

'He ought to understand that the Christmas butter is enough. But every year he sends more and stays less.'

Jade had been surprised that he'd arrived seemingly empty-handed but of course he'd already provided the *things*—the food, the heating, the whole house. All those vital, *practical* things. But then he left. Jade couldn't help wondering what it was that made him feel as if he couldn't stay. Why didn't he want to? Because it wasn't for lack of welcome. Ellen obviously would like nothing more.

'He doesn't like to be a burden.' Ellen sat in a chair at the table and softly offered her opinion on the questions Jade hadn't even voiced. 'He doesn't understand that he never was that to me.'

'What was he?' Jade asked.

'Everything.'

Jade nodded. She could understand how that might be so. But then she heard Ellen draw a breath and she just knew a question was coming. A personal question she had no good answer to. So she got in first to avoid it. 'There are a lot of decorations. Would you like me to see if I can do something with them?'

Ellen took her measure for a long moment. Then she smiled. 'Unlike Alvaro, I never say no to an offer of help. You go for it.'

'Great. Then you go have a coffee with him.' Jade smiled and looked back at the packets of printed paper plates. 'And leave me to this. It'll be fun.'

It *was* fun—because there was an insane amount of Christmas decorations and Jade had never got to do Christmas decorations before. She set the chairs out, having seen the way footmen and maids prepared tables for formal receptions at the palace. She knew the sort of thing that was required. But this was better with all the whimsical little ornaments and snowy glitter to scatter everywhere.

'Uh, Jade?'

She looked up, suddenly self-conscious, and realised Alvaro was standing in the doorway, an odd expression in his eyes.

'I just need a few more minutes,' she said apologetically, glancing down at the table. She'd not realised how extraordinarily colourful she'd made it. 'I'm not quite done yet...'

Had she done an okay job? Or was this...too much?

'Sure thing.' He nodded slowly. 'Come back to the kitchen when you're done. It's looking amazing.'

But he wasn't looking at the table when he said that.

That betraying warmth scalded her cheeks and she looked back down at the paper serviettes. Truth was she'd started off slow purely to give Ellen time with Alvaro, but she'd truly lost track of time. It had been a bigger job than she'd realised.

When she eventually went back to the kitchen she found Alvaro standing, his jacket already on, and teasingly tapping his watch.

'Are you finally ready to leave?' she teased and met his stare limpidly.

'As if it's my fault we're leaving late?'

As Jade walked ahead to the car she heard Alvaro's soft query to the older woman.

'You're okay?' he asked her.

'I'm always okay. But I'm always better for seeing you.'

Jade knew just how she felt.

Alvaro couldn't bear to look at Jade, yet couldn't tear his gaze away—his damn body betrayed him every time. Her stunning hair hung in those half-curls down her back and that emerald jacket with its warm, woolly lining brought out the sparkle in her eyes and the roses in her cheeks. He wanted to grab the lapels, tug her close and taste her again. She looked like a fresh-baked treat—glitter-dusted by all those ludicrous decorations. He wanted to haul her to his hideaway and keep her all to himself like a selfish treasure-hoarding dragon.

And, for just a few nights, he was going to.

He got into the car and waited for her to fasten her seat belt. At least the darkening sky was doing him a favour—he wouldn't be able to see her as she sat beside him. Leaving Ellen's almost two hours later than planned shouldn't matter. He should be relieved to have less time completely alone with Jade and be pleased to have spent more time helping out Ellen. But Jade had had more time with Ellen too and her super-polite reticence had almost instantly melted, revealing her innate warmth and humour.

'Thanks for being so patient with Ellen,' he said gruffly.

'Why wouldn't I be?' Jade sounded surprised. 'It was a privilege to meet her.'

He found he couldn't say anything to that. Ellen was the most important person in his life. But he was deeply private and protective towards her. So someone seeing, someone knowing? But Jade wasn't just someone. And she was precious too. Even when he didn't want her to be.

'Did you think I would find it a chore?' Her voice cooled.

An ache bloomed in his chest. He'd not meant to offend her. 'I figure you have to meet people all the time. It must get tiring.'

'I might not find it naturally easy, but I do try.'

Oh, she did. And whether she found it easy or not, she was good at it. She listened and set people at ease. 'You were lovely with her.' He forced himself to smile and lighten the mood. 'But dressing the Christmas table, Jade?'

'I thought you and Ellen might like some time to catch up without me.'

Yeah, he'd suspected she'd fiddled about with those decorations as a stalling tactic so Ellen could talk with him longer—asking everything but those questions that really mattered. They both knew to avoid those. But Jade had wanted more time for them. Because Jade was very sweet.

'You didn't need to do that,' he muttered, a little hoarse. 'Ellen and I understand each other perfectly well.'

'It was fun,' she parried lightly.

Yeah, she *had* enjoyed it. He'd seen that when he'd gone to find out what was taking her so long—he'd been unable to resist quietly spying on her. She'd taken such care and such sweet joy, becoming self-conscious only when she'd realised how long she'd taken. She'd joked about making origami animals from paper towels, but he'd seen the pleasure she'd found in setting out gaudy dollar-shop decorations and hanging tinsel as if she'd never touched it before. And she possibly hadn't—not up close, not to play with herself. Even in their poorest moments Ellen had found a string of tinsel from somewhere and Alvaro never let her go without yards of it now. Ellen had struggled on her own for so long and he owed everything to her. And for once it was easier to talk about her rather than think about the other woman currently sitting beside him.

'I've tried to get her into a new place,' he said. 'But she won't move. I changed her appliances though. Haven't heard the end of it. Her baking has suffered ever since, apparently.'

Jade chuckled.

'She's useless at accepting help.' He smiled fondly. 'Fiercely independent, to the point of frustration. But she worked so hard for so long and never got ahead. It wasn't her fault. There just weren't the hours in the day and by the time she took me on, she was tired. In my early teens I realised that getting her out of that hand-to-mouth cycle was down to me. She was worn down from all those years working all those hours to support others. Her own family. Her mother. Her brother. Then me.'

She should've had someone who'd helped her long before him. And he'd been part of the burden holding her down for too long already.

'And you did that, right? She doesn't have to work any more if she doesn't want to.'

She still did, of course. He nodded.

'You keep her house maintained, you stock her pantry.'

'She gives most of it away. She takes in all manner of waifs and strays and I worry she'll get taken advantage of again.'

'Again?'

That 'family' of hers had more than taken advantage. They'd used her up, literally worn her out. It had only been when she'd taken Alvaro that she'd finally fully escaped them. When she'd seen what they'd done to him.

'She gives too much,' he said in vague explanation.

'Is that possible?'

'When it's at your own expense—yes.' It had cost Ellen—her youth, her time, her health, her own future.

'So you only see her on Christmas Eve,' she said softly. 'You don't go to her dinner on the day?'

'I don't want to add to her load. It's really just another job for her, only this time the restaurant is at her home. I don't understand why she still does it when she doesn't have to. Why she wants all the work of cooking for a bunch of people she doesn't really know. You'd think she'd want a break.'

'Maybe she appreciates the break from the financial stress, sure. But perhaps there are other things she gets out of it? Being needed…caring for someone or something. That's important to a lot of people.'

'Not to me,' he muttered. He refused to allow it to be. 'I owe Ellen and I'll always support her and I'll support my employees. But beyond that?'

He needed his space and his freedom. He glanced sideways and saw the pure scepticism on her face. 'You don't believe me?'

'I don't believe for a second that you don't care.'

'Well, you're wrong.' As he rejected her no-tion a bitter bubble formed right below his ribs and forced him to challenge her back. 'Who do you care for?'

'My country.'

His lips twisted. 'One person's not enough for you? You need a whole nation?'

'Apparently,' she answered lightly.

'You and Ellen,' he murmured softly. 'She won't say no either. Does all things for all people. She won't give up on someone no matter what, and she'll forgive almost anything.'

'Do you forgive?'

That bitter bubble burst, sending that acid through every cell. 'What do you think?'

'I think you forgave Juno's mistake.'

He grunted dismissively. 'I'm not talking that kind of thing. That was nothing.'

'What kind of thing can't you forgive, Alvaro?'

He glanced at her. She'd swivelled in her seat and was studying him too closely. And as he saw the seeking emotion in her eyes he blanched inwardly. He could never tell her all of it. He could never tell anyone. This whole conversation had to be over.

'You should rest, we have quite a drive yet.' He pressed the sound system on the car and sleigh bells rang out.

Thankfully, she took his cue. 'Christmas music?'

'Uh-huh. Cheesy Christmas music. That's what we're doing here, right? Christmas.'

'So you're not working tomorrow?' she asked.

'Guess not.' He swallowed.

He didn't want to think about tomorrow. Or yesterday. Or any time ever. He'd give anything to distract himself from her right now. Because having her here with him, wanting her to like where they were going...holding onto her company longer than he should... It all *mattered*. And he really, *really* didn't want it to matter.

A couple of hours later she saw it and broke the silence.

'Is that a lighthouse?' She sat upright in her seat and stared hard at the building they were heading towards.

He nodded. 'Reactivated after it was restored a few years ago,' he said, glad to focus on something that wasn't personal. 'There are a few private towers along the coastline here—this is one of them. It's not neon, but it is a flashing light. A pretty big one.'

'Is it *yours*?'

'Yeah.'

'That's amazing.' Her face lit up before the lamplight even got to it.

But that bitterness swirling inside him had lodged deep. 'You're not just finding something positive to say?'

'No! Alvaro, this is the coolest thing ever.' She looked back at him and all the light a man could ever want shone in her eyes. 'It's beautiful.'

'It is not a palace, Jade.' He half laughed. But her excitement broke through and pleased him an inordinate amount.

'I don't need a palace. I've spent too long in one of those already.'

And she would be going back to it soon. At least she wasn't going to marry some unworthy aristocrat now. But he half wished she were—that would make her completely forbidden again.

He gripped the wheel, glad of the cover of darkness.

'It's beautiful,' she muttered again softly, leaning forward to see better as he drove down the narrow private road. His road. And for the first time, he wasn't travelling it alone.

The beacon guided him. It had always been a source of peace—like a sanctuary. And it had been gut instinct to bring her with him—that undeniable certainty that she shouldn't be alone this Christmas. Even though he had little to offer her really. But to make up for that, he'd arranged a couple of Christmassy things that he couldn't face right now.

But the *reason* why he couldn't face them was the truth he needed to *avoid* even more.

He couldn't bear to think any more. Or talk. Or do anything other than survive. Because as he parked the car, finally home, he was barely hanging onto his self-control.

Jade walked to the lighthouse cottage beside

him, aware of a terrible tension within him and not understanding why it had suddenly sprung. In silence he swiftly unlocked the door and ushered her in. Aside from the beaming beacon itself, the only other light was from the Christmas tree at the end of the short hallway, so she still couldn't see his face properly. She really needed to see him. But before she could say anything, he caught her hand.

'Come up to the tower,' he muttered.

She followed him up the curling staircase that had been tucked to the left of the door. Around and around she climbed higher, her pulse rising too with every step. It was narrow up there, but—

'This is *incredible*,' she breathed as she took in the bright lamplight and the darkened, wide windows.

There was the sound of sea hitting shore, but the space was otherwise silent. That regular swirl of light offered a sense of strength and safety. It was the ultimate in serene isolation.

But when she turned, she was finally able to see his face and she realised that her sense of safety was very *wrong*.

'Alvaro?'

He stood still and silent and so strong.

'Alvaro?'

'Don't,' he muttered. 'Don't say anything.'

But how could she not say anything when he'd just stripped off his sweater, together with his tee, leaving him bare-chested? How could she not when he moved towards her with such intent?

'What are you doing?' she asked, even though she knew. Even though she wanted it with every ounce of her being. 'I'm leaving soon.'

Her heart pounded as she said it to remind herself too.

'I know,' he muttered. 'That's good.'

'Is it?' She shook her head with a sad little smile.

'Jade...' His voice was rough and gravelly. 'You know I'm right. You know that this can't...'

'I know.'

'And you know we can't not do this now.'

In the sweep of light from the beacon, the intensity in his expression was revealed. She swallowed. The lighter sexiness of that first night had been replaced by something stronger. There was almost ruthlessness in his intent—as if the hunger had deepened and the resulting, revealed pain needed to be assuaged. This time would be different. This time, she truly feared for her heart.

It's too late already.

She closed her mind to that secret whisper. It didn't matter. Because it *was* too late. And because it was too late, there was no denying this now. She lifted her chin and he stepped close to meet her, to cup her jaw in his large, gentle hands. She closed her eyes at the first kiss. She'd missed him. And now she breathed him in—that musky scent, the heat of his body, the surety of his touch.

They barely undressed. They barely had time. There were too many kisses to enjoy and it didn't matter. In the swirl of light that swept over them every other second, they glimpsed all that was needed—desire, willingness, need.

'Please,' she whispered, her arms tight around his shoulders.

He hoisted her into his hold, pressing her back against the wall. Leaning so close she ought to be crushed. Instead she was elated.

'Don't be polite, darling,' he begged. 'Demand what you want from me.'

'What word do you want to hear, if not please?'

He groaned against her and then uttered a command. It was blunt and coarse, yet he whispered it gently in her ear. That was him. An impossible contradiction of demand and patience.

'Do you have any—?'

'Of course.' He slammed the condoms on the wall beside her head. 'I wouldn't hurt you for the world, Jade.'

She was saddened for a second that he considered creating something magical together would be so destructive for them both. But he was right. And then her need overruled everything. 'Hurry, then.'

Because denying him. Denying herself. Was impossible.

Moments later he groaned her name—a long sigh of searing need and looming satisfaction as he slid home.

'You're so ready for me,' he added in an awed whisper.

'I've been ready all week,' she confessed.

'Why didn't you say so sooner? Wasting time.'

'You went away.'

'Ran fast as I could,' he growled and pressed closer still. 'Stupid.'

'Why did you?'

'Because it's like this,' he said simply. 'Too good.' He stared into her eyes as if seeing her for the first time in so long. 'You should get to have all the fun, Jade.'

Did he think so? Right now, *she* thought so too.

'Give it to me, then,' she asked softly.

The flickering light fell on his gorgeous face, his expression burnished in the alternating lamp light and shade of night. They were alone in the world. There was only them, only this. And Jade was utterly lost, utterly captured in his arms, deliciously lost in his intensity, in his tender passion and the brute strength of his body.

CHAPTER ELEVEN

JADE OPENED HER EYES to a beautiful winter's day—the wide window showing the gorgeous blues of the wide ocean and sky. Last night he'd carried her from the tower straight to this big bed. They'd made love for hours. Not had sex—that was not what it had been for her. She'd loved him as hard as she could for as long as she could stay awake. Now she took in the coastal blue and creamy white paintwork, the warmth of natural wool rugs and the worn wooden floor and that low-burning flame of the cosy fire.

It was perfection. And she told herself she could suppress the yearning inside—she'd suppressed pain for a long time before. She could live with an aching heart. She wouldn't let it ruin this couple of days.

'Good morning.' In just black boxers and nothing else, he was a gift.

But he'd brought her coffee too; she could smell the invigorating strength of it and see the steam curling from the blue mug.

'Merry Christmas,' she whispered, curling her toes at the sight of him.

'Shh.' He bent and gently silenced her with a touch of his finger to her lips. 'Not yet.'

'No?' She frowned.

He shook his head and laughed. 'First we start with an Easter egg hunt.'

'A…*what*?' She raised herself up on two elbows as he sat on the edge of the bed beside her.

'Easter egg hunt.' He looked at her blandly.

'You…' She cocked her head to study him more closely. 'It's *Christmas*.'

'Yeah, but I figure, if you didn't really get a Christmas, I bet you didn't get Easter either. Or Halloween. Obviously not Valentine's Day…'

'Obviously…' Her heart thudded and she couldn't help but slide into the warmth of his smile.

'So. We might not do them in the exact right order…but an Easter egg hunt.'

His playfulness astounded her. So did the lighthouse's cottage. In the course of the hunt for gold-foil-wrapped chocolate decadence, she discovered the other decorations gilding the beautifully refurbished cottage. So many decorations. There was Christmas in the kitchen. Valentine's in the bathroom—champagne and a giant heart balloon above the bath, which had that amazing view across the ocean. She peeked in to discover Halloween in the study with a witch's hat and a cauldron and a carved pumpkin jack-o'-lantern on the side table next to a plush reading armchair. At each of these small decorated settings sweet treats were stationed. The effort and thought he'd gone to put a lump in her throat.

'Alvaro…'

'Silly, I know.'

'Not silly.' She faced him and slung her arms around his neck. 'I love that there are themed snacks in every room for us to refuel.'

'Holiday candy can't be beaten.' He tugged her closer. 'And I'm glad you got my plan. Season's Eatings.'

But she didn't eat. She kissed him. Lazily and playfully and with such sweet gratitude—showing rather than saying how his gesture made her feel. He'd put in so much effort. Already the fires were lit in the bedroom, kitchen and study, making the whole cottage gorgeously warm.

'This must have taken you ages.' She hugged his arm as she gazed around again in absolute awe.

He laughed. 'I'd love to take the credit, but it only took me a few phone calls. I have a person who checks on the place and he got a party company to deck it out. I had to hide most of it from you last night.' He shot her a look. 'I paid them very well given it is the holiday season, but they didn't seem to mind.'

'I bet they had a blast.' Who wouldn't want to come to this magical place?

After the hunt, as they snacked on the Easter eggs they'd found, he pointed out the two stockings hanging on the Christmas tree that she'd not yet noticed.

'Alvaro…' She suddenly felt dreadful; she had no gift for him.

'Don't panic.' He chuckled as he caught the distressed look she shot him. 'This isn't from me. It's from Ellen.'

Jade's heart beat a flood of warmth around her body. She reached into the felt stocking and pulled out a gorgeous soft green winter hat.

'Knitting is her hobby—though she's slower now. She has a collection she chose from.'

'I love it.' She was so touched.

'She chose well,' he said softly. 'It matches your eyes.'

'What did you get?' She peered eagerly.

His was a matching soft wool hat, only in dark grey.

'It looks good on you.' She giggled. Especially with just the boxers he had on.

'Why don't you go into the study? I'll be there in a moment.'

She'd already decided the study was her favourite room—aside from the bedroom, of course—with its stunning views of the ocean, and the cosy comfort of its whitewashed walls, bookcases and plump, soft furniture.

Two minutes later Alvaro appeared carrying a tray, on top of which was a gorgeous chocolate cake and a single lit candle.

'What's this?' She stood to meet him.

'I thought, if the main festival days were impersonal, what were birthdays like in recent years?' He looked at her gently. 'I had a hunch that maybe not all queens got to eat cake?'

Her heart melted all over again at his astuteness. And his consideration.

'No.' Her birthday had barely registered on her father's mind.

She'd missed her sister and her mother so much at those times. Once they'd left there'd been nothing personal—a brief greeting from her father, a signed book, and a reminder to stay calm and study hard.

'So we're having cake for breakfast?' she asked. 'Because it's a treat day?'

'Why not, right? It's Christmas.'

It certainly was. Jade's heart filled as he sank into the big armchair by the fire and watched her, a smile on his face as she blew out the candle.

'Did you make a wish?' he asked.

'I'm not telling,' she teased. She carefully cut into the cake with the enormous knife he'd brought with him and marvelled as a mountain of candy-covered chocolate pieces cascaded out, spilling all over the pretty plate. A couple of pieces even hit the floor.

'Oh, wow!' She giggled. 'That's awesome.'

She could see the chocolate cake itself was rich and decadent and then with that mess of colour in the centre?

'It's the birthday cake I would have adored as a kid,' he said softly.

Her heart burst and she turned to face him. 'Would have?'

Alvaro shrugged as he watched Jade carefully put a slice of cake on a small plate. The flush in her cheeks, the smile that hadn't left her face since she'd woken, they were the best presents he'd ever had. She didn't cut a second slice, instead she came with the plate and fork and, with a wriggle of her hips, wordlessly asked to sit on his lap. She was the sexiest thing. He teased the thin strap of her negligee as she settled over his thighs and offered him a bite. How could he resist?

'You like?' she asked.

Somehow it had flipped, as if he were the one receiving the gift—yet he wasn't quite comfortable. He should be pleased and at ease. He'd checked on Ellen, he'd come to his sanctuary, he had Jade back in his bed and she'd loved his little 'festival of festivals'. Now he had cake and warmth and the most beautiful woman in the world on his knee.

Yet the strangest wall of emotion slammed into

him—hitting him so off track, he couldn't even figure what it was. As it sank beneath his skin, he felt exposed and somewhat mortified that he'd done this at all. And now? Now she was looking at him with gleaming eyes and a smear of chocolate just below her sweet lower lip and—

'It's gorgeous,' he muttered.

His body ached and it shouldn't. It ought to be sated and in some soporific state of recovery, yet now he hungered for things more than physical. It hurt. His chest, his gut. It really, really hurt.

'You didn't ever get a cake like this?' she asked gently as she offered him another bite.

'You know I didn't,' he said huskily.

A frown gathered in her eyes. 'But I'm sure Ellen did something?'

He heard the curiosity in Jade's voice, saw it in her eyes.

'Ellen did her best. Always.' He couldn't say anything more.

Ellen was a carer; she'd taken in the most unwanted of unwanted things. More than stray dogs or waifish children, but the absolute rejects. She'd been tough but she'd had to be. They wouldn't have survived otherwise.

Jade was watching him. Sure, the basic details were out there—he'd been given up for an adoption that hadn't worked out and Ellen had taken him in. But the specifics hadn't been that straightforward. He didn't ever go into those. And yet here those details were, cramming in his head—memories of birthdays and Christmases gone by in which there'd been…anger and hurt and rejection and such loneliness.

He wanted to tear his gaze away from her. He wanted to clear his throat. He wanted to escape…yet he couldn't move. And he certainly couldn't speak. He couldn't tell her the whole of it. He'd never told anyone. Not even he and Ellen had discussed it. It was in the past, long, long buried.

In the end Jade glanced away, faint colour running under her skin. She caught sight of the whiteboard on the wall above his desk and seized on it. 'You were serious about this usually being a strategy day?'

He rested his head back on the chair and gently stroked her back, unable to resist the contact. It soothed him even though every time he touched her it was as if his vital organs got an electric shock.

'Companies don't run by themselves,' he said. 'I need to check direction, and there's inevitably some crisis or other to prepare for…'

'Yet you continue to expand?' She turned back to face him. 'You don't think you have enough?'

He half smiled at her as he shook his head. It wouldn't ever be enough and, no, he couldn't ever rest.

'Do you worry that one day you'll wake up and it'll all be gone?' she asked softly.

He stiffened. He'd worked hard for what he had and he wasn't about to lose it. 'I'm not really that much of a risk-taker, Jade.' He'd had to be to begin with, but not any more. 'You've seen it yourself. I keep my safe reserves.'

And he was always, always hungry. He didn't really mean for food or indeed sex. But for that security. Because he always felt that threat looming. He had to keep winning. He knew what happened when you lost. When you no longer had any tangible value.

He picked up the fork and fed her a piece of the cake to stop her asking another question. Yet stupidly he couldn't help from admitting the tiniest truth to her.

'When I was little, my birthday was never celebrated. It was nothing to be celebrated.' Back then he'd only known what day it even was, thanks to Ellen. 'Ellen made me a cupcake once, when I was nine.'

He remembered it clearly. And the repercussions when the others had found out.

Jade was very still on his lap; he could feel her sudden tension. But her eyes had such light to them—they were so clear and vibrant and he couldn't look away from her even when it seemed that she was looking right into him and seeing the gnarled lump of nothing inside. 'You knew her then?' she prompted so softly.

'I've known her all my life,' he admitted simply and the long-sealed vat of poison bubbled up, bursting through the crust he'd thought indestructible. And he couldn't stop it. 'My birth mother was young. Her very uptight parents were horrified and the only reason I was even born was because by the time my existence was discovered, it was too late for me not to be.' He rested his head on the high-backed chair. 'She was so young she didn't even realise she was pregnant. Not too young to have a boyfriend from the wrong side of the tracks, though. A boy her father couldn't have disapproved of more. So, I was given up.'

'Adopted?'

'Not through the usual channels unfortunately. My grandfather didn't want anyone to know, so they sent my mother away and the second I was born they gave me to Nathan and Lena. Nathan had once worked for him—so it was a private arrangement. They were paid to take me, on the condition that there would never be any communication between my birth family and me. Certainly, there would never be any contact between me and my mother. My connection to the whole family would be denied.'

Jade's jewel-like eyes softened. Of course, she understood the pain of that—she'd experienced similar in her life with her own mother.

He knew she hated being kept in the dark. And she'd shared her secrets with him. What did it matter for her to know she wasn't alone? And it was because of that—and the softness in her expression—that more spilled from him.

'My birth wasn't even registered at the time. But later on, there was contact,' he said wryly. 'Because Nathan and Lena only took me for that monthly pay-cheque. They weren't interested in *me*, I was just a complete pain. Nor were they interested in working… They only wanted their next fix. They both left all the cooking and cleaning and caring for me to Nathan's older half-sister.'

It took her only a moment. 'Ellen.'

'She did everything. She had done all her life. Everything for everyone. She'd left school early to care for her mother, who got unwell after Nathan's birth, so she didn't get a decent education. When their mum died, Ellen struggled to raise Nathan. He took huge advantage of her for years. Lena then did the same—they treated her like their slave. And they used her to look after me. And she was so…worn, so downtrodden with years of that awful treatment, she just accepted it all.' It had frustrated the hell out of him. 'But then the monthly money to cover my costs stopped coming. So one day, when Ellen was at work, Lena and Nathan took me back to my grandfather's house to find out why.'

The bitterest, smallest details spilled out. 'It was my ninth birthday when I met my grandfather for the first and last time.'

Jade sat so still on his lap he didn't think she

was even breathing. He wasn't sure he was either. He couldn't—because every pulse point in his body hurt.

'He wasn't interested, of course. He was irate. Yelling that he didn't want to see them *or* me. He'd screwed up some investment. Screwed up his marriage. Sure as hell screwed up his daughter. In the end he just slammed the door. As far as Nathan and Lena were concerned, if there was no money, they didn't want me any more. So they left me there—outside his locked gates. My grandfather didn't open them. So I was alone.'

He'd been terrified, because the only people he'd known there had driven off, leaving him in some city miles away from the one person who'd ever shown him any kindness.

'What happened?' Jade asked.

'Ellen came when she realised what had happened.'

'How long were you waiting?'

'I don't know,' he muttered. 'Hours. She didn't have a licence let alone a car. She had to bus and then walk and she'd only found out after she'd been at work all day. When she'd forced it out of a drugged-up, barely coherent Nathan.'

'You must have been terrified.'

'Cold and confused and starving.' The memories twisted inside. 'Ellen had made me that cupcake in the morning, but Nathan saw and before she left for work, he raged at her for wasting an egg on me. I was nothing but a drain on them then, you see. He smashed it in front of me after she'd gone. He was just so bloody *mean*.' Alvaro had hated him. 'But then, when it was dark, she came.' Finally, finally, he'd been too relieved to even cry. 'We never went back. She walked out on Nathan and Lena. She was finally furious enough to get past her own fear. Not for what they'd done to her. But to me. You should have heard how they used to talk to her. I'll never forget it.'

'And how did they talk to you?'

Yeah, he didn't forget that either. How unwanted he'd been. How useless. How, if he wasn't bringing them money, he wasn't worth anything.

'Ellen worked every job she could—taught me how a work ethic enabled a person to survive. Cooking, cleaning, picking crops, bussing tables, stocking supermarket shelves in the small hours... and she wasn't young then, Jade. And it was hard and some days there was nothing much to make a meal with. And I was so hungry.'

'So you worked hard too.'

He nodded. But he'd been on his own a lot—learning to cook as best he could, not just for himself, but for Ellen too. So she had something to come home to.

'My birth mother had been a kid who made a mistake. But her parents? They were wealthy and they could have afforded to do the right thing. They could have gone through a proper adoption agency or something. But they were too obsessed with their own perfect image. So they passed her little mistake—*me*—off to someone else—never taking responsibility, let alone any kind of care for anyone other than themselves.'

'What happened to her—your birth mother?'

'No clue.' He shrugged.

'And her boyfriend?'

'Apparently they paid him off too. My grandfather told me he took the money and didn't look back.'

'You've never tried to trace him?'

'I don't want to know,' he said bluntly. 'I don't need that rejection all over again. Ellen and I got through—we got out of it. I've never seen any of them again and I never, ever want to.'

'Alvaro, I'm so sorry.'

'I'm not,' he said, meaning it completely. 'Not any more. I don't need people like that in my life. People who only want to use you? Who're only interested when you have something to offer them—like money. Or status. People who can't stand there and take responsibility for their own damn actions.'

Jade looked upset and angry and he shouldn't have told her. But once he'd started he'd been unable to stop and now she was…

'They should have been more to you,' she said with a broken voice. 'They should have been there for you. They should have supported you.'

He shook his head. 'Having it hard made me better. Made me fight in a way that maybe I wouldn't have if everything had come easily. It made me appreciate Ellen and work my ass off to get her what she deserved.'

'What you deserved too.'

Yeah. Becoming strong, becoming independent, had been everything. He'd refused to be a 'burden' to anyone any more. He would repay Ellen a million times over. And he would always make his own way with full independence. And he would never, ever *need* anyone again the way he'd needed someone that day when he'd been abandoned.

Only now Jade was watching and to his absolute horror a need deep within him was unfurling...for *her*. He needed her. Right now.

To lose himself in, right? To find that mindless obliteration in sex with her. Because he didn't want—*couldn't* want—to need her any other way.

But he couldn't seem to move; his body was leaden. And his damned head hurt. Not just his head. His heart too. Everything. It all still hurt.

She carefully took the plate from him and picked up the black witch's hat that had been placed there as that stupid Halloween decoration, putting it on her head to make room for the plate.

He nodded, because it was perfect. She did bewitch him. And that was all this was, wasn't it? An ephemeral thing that wasn't even real. She was like a beautiful witch. She looked at him unlike any other woman he'd known too. There was heat certainly, but tenderness too. None of that avariciousness in her eyes, no awareness of any kind of quid pro quo, it was almost an innocence. It was, he finally realised, an authenticity. And now she curled into him, wrapping her arms around him, holding him in an embrace that he couldn't help returning. Enfolding his arms around her, feeling her soft skin and warm body, her gentle breath on his chest and the regular beat of her loving heart.

He should move, but he couldn't. She was like an anchor in his lap. Not letting him leave. Giving him something to hold onto. Herself. Just to hold, here and now. And suddenly he was so very tired. He'd kept all that in, all his life. And now?

He'd never been as exhausted. As aching. And as *okay*. It was the strangest feeling of release.

'Do you know what you are?' Her whisper was so faint he had to concentrate hard to hear her. 'All my birthdays and Christmases, rolled into one perfect present.'

Oh, but that was what she was for him. Unburdened by her crown, she was just Jade. And her gift to him was just herself. Not just her body, but her care too. He felt it flowing from her now. Everything.

'No,' he muttered as that most vulnerable part of his soul shrank from the burn of her tenderness.

But she rested her head on his shoulder and wouldn't let him go. 'I won't hurt you,' she whispered.

He should have scoffed at that soft promise, should have teased—*as if she could?*

Instead he closed his eyes and wished he could believe her.

CHAPTER TWELVE

ALVARO SLOWLY STIRRED the risotto, taking the time
to make it creamy and rich and telling himself
everything was just fine. It was only Christmas.
Only a day in which there'd been a few smiles,
a lot of sex, few words spoken. And what were
words, after all? Mere moments that vanished with
the next breath.

But he couldn't believe the words he'd uttered
today. He never thought about his past, let alone
raked it up and told someone else of that miserable, lonely rejection. But, he rationalised as he
swirled figures of eight with the wooden spoon,
she was about the one person in the world he could
trust. A queen—keeper of total calm and self-
containment. She was ultra-discreet in her own
life and so wary of exposing anything to anyone
for fear of it being splashed across the media. She
was resolute. And he respected her for that even
though it annoyed him on an intimate level. But
he knew he didn't need to worry that she wouldn't
keep his past private. His knowledge of her true

identity was the secret that bound them both to confidence.

So it wasn't a fear of someone else knowing. No. The mistake he'd made ran deeper than some mere switch or even some mere affair. And it was more dangerous. Somehow her knowing, her seeing him, her *soothing* him had struck a vein within. And now that vein wanted to bleed even more.

The raw exposure was hideously uncomfortable. The irony was he'd *wanted* to tell her at the time. At the time it had actually felt good. He'd felt a deep peace after for all of...what...*all of the time you had her in your arms*.

For the first time in his life he'd fallen asleep on Christmas Day—slept half the afternoon away, like a damn baby. Cuddling her. And when he'd finally stirred, she was still there. She'd lifted her head and smiled at him and he'd done the only thing he possibly could.

He'd kissed her. Silencing, not just her, but the voice in his head telling him he didn't deserve it...that he shouldn't allow it...because that other part of him, that long-ignored, tiny, tiny part was more desperate than anything for it to happen. For him to take what she offered. All she offered. Again and again like a glutton, because he'd been deprived too long. Like the damaged, undeserving man he was.

And for as long as he was touching her, it had

been okay. But now? Now there was something akin to panic. But he couldn't suck it back. He couldn't *untell* her everything. He couldn't cut off the connection that had somehow been forged.

It doesn't matter.

Because she was leaving. And this would end. She was the queen of a small country on the other side of the world. They would have nothing to do with each other again after she returned home in only a few short days. This was merely an interlude for them both.

But now, as he reminded himself of that, his panic magnified.

He should end it now. But he couldn't. He shouldn't have let any of this happen and yet he still couldn't resist, still couldn't refuse himself these moments.

He carried two bowls of the risotto up to the tower. She was curled in a chair up there, looking out at the coastline as the sky began to darken and the beacon began its work. Her smile was quick when she saw him and he desperately needed distraction before he sank to his knees and spilled out the rest of his soul to her. Somehow she knew. She made light jokes about the juxtaposition of cheap candy and rich chocolate. And in the end there was nothing he could do but haul her close again. He was determined to expend every ounce of this desire. But no matter how many hours he spent with her in his arms it deepened still. Even when, beyond exhaustion, he still wanted her close.

It seemed the guy could do everything. He wasn't just strong and skilled, he was thoughtful—treating her to gourmet cakes and trashy take-out food, then cooking her a beautiful dinner. Making her move, making her laugh. And finding out the heartache he'd suffered had only made her appreciate his strength even more. The loneliness and the rejection that had given him such drive made her ache to her bones.

But he'd built a world for himself. He had not just a career but a whole company and ambition beyond. He'd made this his sanctuary, his security. She understood he needed freedom and independence. But in reality, he'd cemented his own isolation. Having glimpsed his background, she understood why. The problem—and it was *her* problem—was that she'd fallen in love with him. Deeply, completely in love with him.

She waited for a while—letting herself float through the next two days—hoping this emotion was just a wave of hype and hormones, a feeling that would pass like any other given enough space and time. Jade was used to managing emotions, she knew how to live with deep ones, how to keep them secret, how to mask them.

But this? This was too big, too raw, too unwieldy. She couldn't contain this; couldn't stop this; couldn't cope with it for too much longer. And while she knew he wanted her, he didn't *need* her. And she certainly didn't think he loved her. He was too controlled for that.

And even if he did, this couldn't go anywhere.

She needed to do what was best not just for her country. But for him too. And in this instance, yes, her own desires had to come behind his.

She couldn't ask him to live a life of restriction and duty in the way she had to. She couldn't ask him to sacrifice so much. He'd resent her eventually—as her mother had resented her father. And no way could they maintain a long-distance relationship either. She'd lived through separation with Juno and it was too hard to have someone you loved so far away for so much of the time. It would hurt her heart too badly.

So it was better to be over completely. And as soon as possible.

The conversation between them stayed light, but terribly fragile. It was as if he, too, was determined to make the most of these moments here. They walked on the beach, laughed about little unimportant things. Mostly they made love like wild animals every moment they could.

And the next morning, it happened.

'Do you mind if we don't drive back to Manhattan?' Alvaro said.

Her bruised heart lifted. 'What did you want to do?'

Did he want to escape somewhere else? Or stay here for ever? Either way she'd have said yes in a heartbeat.

'It's faster if we fly,' he explained.

Her heart plummeted. So stupid. She'd *known* it was coming. Because despite their physical connection, she'd felt him pulling back personally. She had too. They'd had no discussion of his past since Christmas Day, not hers either.

Light and easy. Remember? Light and easy and so very fragile.

It wasn't a long drive to the nearest town and a helicopter charter service there. It wasn't long in the air either. But every second passed like sixty—amplifying the time she had to think. And all the while certainty sank like a lead stone in the lake of her churning stomach acid.

There was only one course of action. She had to go home. She had to say goodbye to him now. Anything difficult was best done sticking-plaster-style—ripping it off in one swift motion. In this case, she decided, it was the *only* way.

From the helicopter port, Alvaro collected a car. She didn't know if he was planning to take her back to his apartment or not, but she knew she had to speak up. Now.

'Can you take me back to Juno's?' she asked as he started the engine. 'I have a couple of things there that I need.'

'Sure, we can go now. It won't take long.'

His easy-going accommodation of her request made her grit her teeth. The drive was familiar now. Her heart raced but she remained cool on the exterior.

As soon as he'd pulled over opposite Juno's apartment she drew in a deep breath.

'Alvaro, I'm going home.'

'You are home.'

'I mean to Monrova. Tonight.'

He killed the engine and swivelled to face her, his eyes wide. 'You're leaving New York tonight?' He looked stunned. 'I thought you had another couple of days—'

'I need to get back to Monrova. Something has…'

She trailed off; she couldn't bring herself to lie to him completely.

'Something has…?' he prompted. 'What something? It's not like you've had any calls—' He gazed at her intently.

She glimpsed emotion in his face. A flash of anger, swiftly smoothed by determined acceptance.

'That's it?' he said. 'That's all you can say?'

But she saw the bitterness of self-blame in his eyes. It was as if he'd expected it all along. And of course he would—she was always going to leave.

But not this soon.

They both knew that. And he took the reason, she realised, to be himself. That this was somehow his fault. She understood why he'd think it—it was what she would think too. Two people who'd been hurt before. Who'd blamed themselves before.

Regret burned the back of her throat. Too late she realised she'd just hurt him. In a way that hadn't needed to happen. He'd done nothing wrong; it wasn't *him*. Suddenly she couldn't leave without telling him her truth. Couldn't let him think she didn't care. Because she did.

Alvaro had been right when he'd said she needed to put herself first sometimes and say what she wanted. But really, he'd meant in sex. He'd not meant for them to become *emotionally* intimate. But they had. And in that too she needed to be brave.

More than that, she needed to do what was *right*.

She gripped the car door handle. She had to *tell* him. She couldn't let him think he wasn't wanted. And she couldn't hold back her own truth. Even though it would change nothing that could happen, it might help him understand. There would be the slightest soothing of her soul too—and hopefully his—just from the power of knowledge.

'I can say more,' she said tightly.

He didn't respond; he just stared at her as if he'd seen Medusa and been turned to stone.

'I have more to say.' Courage began flowing through her veins. 'I have to go now, Alvaro. You want to know why?'

'You've already said why. It's *something*.'

She nodded. 'It's you.'

His eyes dilated.

'Well, to be more correct, it's my feelings for you.'

He was utterly still but already she saw it in his gaze—the denial.

She'd always put duty before desire; protocol before the personal. But her reticence in sharing anything, in admitting anything, in asking for anything, had been more than so-called *duty*. In essence she'd always been afraid. Scared that if she said what she really wanted she'd lose what she loved most. That she'd be sent away—as her mother and her sister had been. But she was leaving now anyway. And speaking her truth wasn't just for him, but for herself too.

'I've fallen in love with you,' she said, amazed at her own calmness. 'I know you joked it might happen. But you weren't being arrogant, in fact you were selling yourself short. You're very easy to fall in love with.' She ran her tongue over her suddenly dry lips. 'You don't have to worry. I'm not proposing. I'm not asking you for a future. I know that's impossible. But I'm telling you how I feel. That's all. I'm trying to be *honest*.'

'No, Jade. I…' He actually looked sorry. 'I don't think this is true.'

'I'm doing the one thing you've encouraged me to do. I'm picking my favourite. And it's you.' Her equilibrium began to tilt. 'Only now you decide you don't want to hear it?'

'You're…' He shook his head. 'You've been very sheltered.'

'Are you about to suggest that I shouldn't trust my own feelings?' She glared at him.

His jaw clenched but he forced a breath. 'I'm about to suggest that you're inexperienced in these things.'

'And you aren't?'

He laughed. Short, bitter, *biting.*

'When did you last have a long-term relationship, Alvaro?' she challenged. 'When did you last open up to anyone?'

His smile vanished.

'Emotional intimacy is something you dodge like a vampire avoiding sunlight,' she snapped.

He stilled, silenced.

'Nothing to say to that?' she asked.

She didn't even want him to say anything now. She just wanted to run away. She didn't know what she'd thought would happen. As if confessing this would *help* in some way? That he might *appreciate* what she'd just *given* him?

Yeah, so wrong on that.

Anger bubbled—like none she'd ever felt.

'So your plan now is to leave?' He shifted in his seat.

She could feel the tension streaming from him. 'Yes.'

'Why?' His cold gaze sliced through her. 'Why

leave early when you've suddenly realised your feelings for me? Why miss out on the few days we have left? Are you too scared to see it through, Jade?' His accusation burned. 'You still don't really believe in your choices yet, do you?'

Why was he being so cruel?

'Because it's going to hurt me,' she said. 'And if I stay 'til the end, it will hurt more.'

'So, you'll admit love in one breath, but run away in the next?'

'It's not like you're perfect.' His antagonism riled her. 'You act like you have it all together. Like you're cool and all in control. You think you have your life just the way you want it and, sure, it's pretty good. To a point. But you're as much of a coward as I am. In fact, more so.'

'How do you figure that?' he snapped.

'Your awesome "independence"? Your whole refusal to be a burden to anyone? It's a cover, so you can hide and not open up, not let anyone in. Because if you let someone in, if you let someone shoulder what you've got going on in there...'

'Then what?' He dared her to say it, frigid rage on his face.

'Then they might leave you.'

He visibly withdrew. That iron anger hardened his amber eyes. 'I think that's *your* fear talking, Jade.'

'Sure. But it's *your* fear too. You choose to be alone. You choose isolation. And it's hurting you.

You should find someone and make your own family.'

'You sound like Ellen.'

'She knows you better than anyone. And she's right,' Jade said. 'You deserve happiness and you should have it all with someone. You shouldn't lock yourself away the way you do.'

'I don't lock myself away. And I don't want a family.'

'Because you don't care?' She shook her head. 'That's *all* you do, Alvaro. *You* are the lighthouse. You're tall and strong and you care for people, you protect them. Like Ellen. Like your employees... But you don't just keep "safe reserves", Alvaro. You also have rocks around you, just like that lighthouse. They're your defence—warning people to stay away from you. Keeping you isolated. But lighthouses aren't fully automated machines, they still need care and attention. They still need a keeper to refuel them. They still need that source of power, at least that *one* person to keep them switched on. *You* need that.'

And so badly she wanted his one person to be her.

'And the irony is,' she said sadly, 'that bright light attracts us all. We're like moths. We want to be around you. To love you. Only you won't let anyone in.'

He didn't just look shocked. He looked horrified. 'Jade...' He paused for a moment, clearly searching carefully for the right words. 'I can't give you what you want.'

And they were the wrong words.

'This was only ever an affair,' he added. 'This wasn't meant to...'

'Become something more?' She knew that this was meant to have been nothing other than an escape for them both. But that didn't explain everything. And, heaven help her, she couldn't stop herself from asking. 'I can't walk away from you without being honest, Alvaro. And I won't allow you to do that either.'

'You won't allow it?'

'*You* encouraged me to speak up for my own desires. To demand what I wanted from you. So tell me.'

'Tell you what?' he suddenly exploded. 'And for what purpose? What *possible* benefit is there to this?'

For all his demands of her, that encouragement of her, *he* didn't talk. And now she was furious.

'*Why* did you do it?' she yelled at him.

'Do *what*?'

'Christmas Day on steroids. Why?'

He gaped. Then breathed. 'I didn't. I told you. I just phoned up a company and they set it all up.'

'At *your* suggestion,' she pointed out, her emotions slipping away again. 'But *you* thought of it. You went to that expense and the effort, because you took the time, you had the consideration. Why did you want to do that for me?'

He glanced away then. 'Maybe it wasn't for you. Maybe it was for me.'

'You?'

'You know I never had those things either.' Frustration ripped out of him. 'We have more in common than you might think, Jade. You had everything, but not the treats. I had nothing, and certainly not the treats. I figured we could both have them for once.'

'And that's all it was?' She didn't want to believe him. She'd wanted it to mean more. For it to have *mattered*.

'You only had three weeks, Jade,' he said, almost plaintively. 'Only a few days. It was your one Christmas of freedom. I wanted to make it good for you.'

'So you only took me there because you knew I was leaving?' she asked. 'You wouldn't have bothered otherwise? With any of it? So, really, it was pity?' He'd done it all because he felt *sorry* for her.

'No. It was a gift.'

A gift? Something nice for the poor, little rich girl?

Christmas Day had just been a favour, a benevolent, charitable act? Hell, it had basically been a *job* for him. And sleeping with her in the first place had been a favour too.

Bitter disappointment broke her heart. *He* broke her heart.

And then she saw it on his face—the apology. She didn't want his *apology*. She wanted his love.

'Jade—'

'It's time for me to leave, Alvaro.' She tried to open the car door but it wouldn't open.

'Jade.'

'Now, Alvaro.' She *needed* him to let her leave.

And this time he listened. The car door locks unclicked. The door swung open. And Jade escaped.

CHAPTER THIRTEEN

THE SALON IN Monrova's Palace Monroyale was still decorated with tall fir trees dressed in scarlet and gold satin ribbons. The same way it had been decorated for the month of December for decades—or at least, for all of Jade's life. Everything was the same—as if she'd never been away or, indeed, never been there at all. She passed the antique furniture knowing she should feel pride in their craftsmanship, their preserved glory...instead they stifled her.

Jade wheeled her trolley case herself, smiling at the footman's astounded expression as he held the door for her.

'Good morning.' She smiled tightly.

'Your Highness.' He blushed as he bowed.

She walked towards the west wing, where her private apartment was situated within the palace.

'Your Highness.' Major Garland halted midway along the wide corridor, a perplexed look wrinkling his very high forehead. 'I thought you were—'

'In Severene, I know.' Jade kept walking. 'I apologise for the confusion.'

'But—' His eyes had bugged almost out of his skull. 'You *are* in Severene, right now. With—'

'Clearly, I'm not,' Jade said crisply. She wasn't about to waste time debating her identity with this supercilious advisor who'd always seemed to sneer at her. 'The princess who is currently in Severene is my twin, Juno. *I* am Jade.'

Major Garland's mouth hung open for an unflattering few seconds. 'But—'

'No buts, Major. It is truly me and if we need to get the palace physician to verify it we can, or you can just take me at my word. Juno and I switched places for a few weeks but I've returned a couple of days earlier than we originally planned.'

'You…what?' A purple hue tinged the expanding frown on Major Garland's face. 'You switched places? As if you're twelve?' He straightened to glower down at her from his full height. 'May I remind you, Princess Jade—?'

'You may not,' she interrupted him. Because calling her 'Princess Jade' revealed exactly what he thought of her. That she was still a child. She wasn't. She was the Queen. And she was also tired and devastatingly heartsore and she grasped for the control expected of her. But, she realised, control didn't mean meekness and mildness. This was a time for honesty and assertiveness and getting what *she* needed—which was support and clarity. Neither of which, she finally realised, she was probably ever going to get from Major Garland. 'I'm the Queen, Major Garland, and I know what my obligations are and I do not need you or anyone else to tell me what I should or should not have done in the past, be doing now or, indeed, do in the future.'

His eyes widened and his mouth hung ajar for another moment. 'But—'

'I need you to gather my senior staff,' she said firmly. She raised her eyebrows at him when he didn't move. 'Now, please, Major.'

'Uh…' He swallowed. 'Of course, Your Majesty. I shall assemble everyone in the Rose Room.'

The Rose Room was a large, cold, uncomfortable conference space where her father had always met with his pompous advisors sitting before— and literally beneath—him at unfriendly rectangular tables. The hierarchy of the palace had been defined by the seating positions. The King himself had sat like some despotic dictator at his own table on a raised platform above them all. Jade had always hated sitting up there for them all to talk to her as if she were still two. 'Actually, I'd prefer not to use the Rose Room for this meeting, thank you, Major.'

His expression puckered as if he'd sucked on something sour. 'But—'

'It's too large and too cold for me. I'd prefer to meet everyone in the dining room.'

'The dining room?' He looked thunderstruck.

She would have laughed if she weren't so cold and tired.

'Yes,' she said, drawing in a calm response. She could keep calm and courteous, she was the *Queen* and she would not shout at any of her people. 'The table is large for us to all fit around. Let's meet in half an hour. We need to summon my assistant back from Severene.' She frowned thoughtfully. 'Actually, leave that to me. I'll sort that when I speak to Juno.'

Minutes later in the privacy of her apartments, she pulled Juno's phone from her pocket and finally turned it on. She'd avoided the task while she'd travelled home. Now she stared at the screen, but there was nothing. No ping, ping, ping of incoming messages. There wasn't even one—let alone any from the one person she wanted to hear from most of all.

Drawing a breath, she touched the keypad and called her sister.

'What's this about you being back in Monrova?' Juno asked instead of even saying hello.

'You've heard already?' Jade shook her head. Major Garland was *very* efficient. 'News travels fast.'

'Is everything okay?' Juno asked.

'More importantly, is everything okay with you?' Jade questioned. 'I heard…'

'I did something stupid,' Juno said quickly. 'But I'm fine. In fact, I'm better than fine...'

Jade gripped the phone, listening closely to her sister's effervescence as she confessed that she hadn't just 'jumped' King Leonardo. She'd fallen in love with him and he had with her. The joy was something Jade hadn't heard in her sister's voice in so long and she loved it. They planned to marry as soon as possible, meaning Juno would become the queen that Jade had always known her sister was capable of being. It was perfect and *everything* that Jade needed right now.

'You're going to live near.' Jade's eyes filled with the sweetest relief. 'You're going to be my neighbour.' It was a balm soothing her own devastation.

'Jade?' Juno suddenly paused. 'Is everything okay?'

'Better than okay.' Jade made herself nod. 'It was just time for me to come home. I'm ready, Juno, really ready to be here and do this the way I actually want to. I had a great time away. It was so good for me.'

None of that was a lie. She couldn't regret a moment of it. But she heard Juno's hesitation and her intake of breath and knew she was going to ask something difficult and unavoidable.

'Now, when's the wedding going to be?' Jade spoke again quickly to head off Juno's query.

She knew her sister could hear something in

her voice. Even when they'd spent so many years apart, they could tell—there was no real ability to lie to each other. To conceal, yes, but not outright lie. So she had to distract. Fortunately, Juno fell for it, her happiness swamping her—making it impossible for her not to answer and share her joy.

Jade listened with pure delight and then they quickly made plans to front up to the press. The only way forward for them both was with honesty.

The irony that everything she'd done to save her sister's job was now rendered utterly pointless wasn't lost on Jade. She didn't even need to *tell* Juno about anything that had happened in New York. Certainly nothing about Alvaro. She couldn't anyway; she didn't want to say anything that would cause Juno to worry about her. She would let nothing diminish her sister's much-deserved happiness.

Juno and Leonardo the couple came as no real surprise. Jade had suspected there was something between them from the moment she'd seen those photos from the Monrova Winter Ball. And now, listening to Juno, she knew they brought the best out in each other. Some things were just meant to be.

She and Alvaro, however, were not.

He'd caught her eye from the first second—he was compelling and magnificent. But then, when he'd let her in? Let her really see him? Not just feel him, not just touch him, but be with *him*—his intelligent and laughing, protective and vulnerable, utterly passionate self?

But Alvaro hadn't argued, hadn't begged her to stay, hadn't really said anything when she'd told him she loved him. And he certainly hadn't wanted to hear what she'd finally been brave enough to say. And that hurt her deeply. She'd never said that to *anyone* before.

While on the one hand he'd given her so much—a joie de vivre and an inner confidence she'd been missing—he'd also devastated her. Because she wanted everything else from him too. She wanted *him*. And for the briefest of moments, she'd thought he wanted her too.

But he didn't.

The afternoon she returned to Monrova—having liaised with Leonardo and Juno, and with her assistant back by her side to help—she read her prepared statement to the teleprompter. She'd watched King Leonardo make his statement and then take a couple of questions only moments before her live cross. Beside him, Juno had looked beautiful—she was literally glowing. It was the only thing that got Jade through the broadcast.

What got her through the next couple of days was pure grit. She called on Serena, her assistant to work through switching up her daily schedule and her long-term commitments, finally changing some of the routine that her father had imposed on her life for so long. Finally, she felt liberated and able to make her own calls. Hiring a new personal trainer was going to be one of them, she laughed at herself. Calm but nervous, questioning herself but with growing confidence in her own choices, she began. *She* was going to be okay—eventually. Because she'd found her own voice.

But at night her mind wandered and she remembered things that were so wonderful, but so bad for her. She'd asked for what she wanted from Alvaro. Repeatedly. And he'd given it to her. He'd listened. He'd not minimised her desires as the irascible wishes of a spoilt princess, but seen them for what they were—the real, secret desires of a lonely woman who'd wanted to *feel* something for once. Who'd yearned to be wanted in return.

She'd been such a fool about that bit. He'd just been giving her the fairy tale for a fortnight. Because, for just a fortnight, he could. He could deliver every desire, every dream…because it was finite and it was only physical. Because there was not and never would be a future in it. And that was safe for him, wasn't it?

But the second she'd suggested that there might be a future?

That was when he'd pulled back. Because he hadn't meant any of it. He *had* just been indulging her. *Spoiling* her. Like the poor little rich royal she was.

For the first time she understood why people did such stupid things for lust. It fogged the mind and got so far beneath your skin, it made you reckless. It felt so good, you didn't care about possible dangers or consequences or repercussions. She imagined it was like a drug.

Jade hadn't been an addict before. Hadn't craved anything the way she craved physical contact with Alvaro. His touch. His kiss. His care and attention. She missed it. He'd so arrogantly teased her that she'd fall for him. But it wasn't *him*, was it? Wasn't it just his body? The way he could make her feel? A physical response?

But it wasn't. Because the physical frustration she could survive. The tear in her heart and in her soul?

She liked herself more when she was with him. Being around him, she felt free to say what she wanted, without having to be polite about it. People had looked at her all her life. They'd stared—endlessly. But no one looked at her the way he looked at her. As if he really saw her— the soft, secret, most vulnerable, most human part of her. And no one had wanted to listen the way he wanted to either. She'd trusted him. And in the end, she'd trusted him with everything. She'd trusted him with her heart.

That was when he'd let her down. But even then, when she was honest with herself, she knew he hadn't. It wasn't his fault he didn't want to carry that burden. She'd been wrong even to ask him. Hadn't she seen how terrible it was for someone to be caught here—in the palace—when the relationship wasn't right? And it had been less than a fortnight—to be irrevocably changed by one person?

And even if he had been—even if by just a fraction of the way she had? It made no difference to the inevitable impossibility of *them*. His company was everything to him as her country was everything to her. There could be no compromise. It wouldn't be fair on either of them.

But as it was, he'd *not* been changed. At the end of the day, he didn't care for her the way she did for him.

He had not fallen in love with her.

Alvaro's phone rang. He glanced at the screen and grimaced. This was one call he couldn't decline.

'Hey, Ellen.' He braced for incoming attitude.

'I've just seen that friend of yours on the television.'

Yeah, he'd seen it too. Over and over. But Ellen had obviously only just caught up with it on the late-night news show.

'She's a queen, Alvaro. You didn't tell me that.'

'I know.'

He didn't want to talk about her. Didn't want to think about her. But he'd been unable to do anything else for hours. Seeing her at that press conference—all regal in the palace courtyard—she'd looked so different, so distant. Monrova was a whole world away from him.

Ellen was quiet. Yeah, they didn't talk about the things that hurt. What was the point?

'How was Christmas dinner?' he asked heavily. 'All those potatoes get eaten?'

'Every one.' Another long pause. 'Alvaro?' Ellen mumbled. 'Are you okay?'

She'd named him, this woman. She'd raised him. She'd protected him. She'd done the best she could, as he had for her. It sure as hell hadn't been perfect. But after their escape, at least, it had definitely been better than okay.

But no. He wasn't okay now. He was angry. Jade had turned everything upside down. Jade had made him want. She'd made him wonder. And she'd made him dream.

Distant, unattainable, *impossible* dreams.

And he couldn't even go to the lighthouse to escape any more.

'I'm fine, Ellen,' he lied. Because there was no way he could burden her with the truth. Not when she'd done everything she could for him already. This was his own agony to endure. 'I need to go. I have a meeting I can't miss. I'll call you later.' But there was one thing he suddenly realised he needed to admit—one fact she deserved to hear. And had deserved to hear for years. One thing neither of them ever admitted.

'Thanks for calling.' The words choked in his throat. 'I love you, Ellen.'

There was another silence. 'I love you too.' She sounded as rusty as he had.

Alvaro ended the call and pressed his phone to his aching chest and figured maybe Jade would've been pleased.

And maybe he could get used to saying such things.

CHAPTER FOURTEEN

'I WOULD PREFER the trinity tiara, Major Garland.'

'Are you sure? Your father, the King, preferred—'

'The crown of Monrova is too heavy for me on a sustained walkabout.' She already had a slight headache; she didn't need to make it worse. She saw the Major pause, but she spoke again before he could. 'I'm sure you'll agree.'

'Of course, ma'am.'

'Thank you.'

Within half an hour the tiara was delivered to her suite from the Royal Jewel House. Jade sat patiently as her maid styled her hair around it. The waiting crowd was larger than usual this year. They were curious about the twin switch. There had been some criticism in the press, but she'd had a swathe of public support online as people defended her right to have a private holiday away. And everyone was entranced by Leonardo and Juno—their happiness simply radiated all the way here from Severene. They were the perfect fairy tale.

But today marked the end of Jade's holiday period and her royal obligations resumed, beginning with the New Year's Day message and a brief walkabout just beyond the palace gates. It was the first chance her people had to see her since that media conference of a couple of days ago.

When it was time, Jade took a minute to calmly breathe before stepping out beyond the palace wall and into the small arena in the centre of her city. Immediately the crowds cheered. Their sonic wall of warmth lifted her spirits. She squared her shoulders and her smile came naturally—more openly with the more people she greeted. Finally, she settled in.

'Thank you for coming out in this cold.' She spoke softly to well-wishers while her assistant gathered their offered bouquets.

'Lovely to have you back, Queen Jade.'

'It's lovely to be home.' She beamed, appreciating how true her response was.

She was here, doing what she'd been born to do. And she would do it her way. She walked along the barrier that had specially been erected, taking the time to talk to as many people as she could.

Towards the end of her time a prickle of awareness skated over her skin. Turning, she scanned the crowd, having the oddest sensation of being watched.

Duh. Of course, you're being watched.

But it felt as if *Alvaro's* gaze were upon her. That electrified sizzle swept over her skin. But he was so tall, he'd literally stand above most others and she'd spot him—wouldn't she—if he were here?

No. That was the stuff of films and fantasies—pure wishful thinking. He was on the other side of the world, working on his strategic plans, all alone in his lighthouse. Right where he wanted to be. So she smiled again and, with a final wave, allowed her security team to sweep her back inside.

She swiftly returned to her private apartment. Later this afternoon she'd arrange a meeting to reorganise her schedule. She'd felt briefly invigorated from that interaction with the public, and she wanted more of it. But right now, she was eager to get out of her dress and tiara and have a moment to breathe again.

She didn't get it. Her phone rang a bare three seconds after she'd dismissed her maid and closed the door. It was her own mobile phone—she'd had Juno's one couriered back to her, not wanting to stare at it in the hope Alvaro might call. And it was her twin ringing now.

'Juno?' Jade answered briskly. 'Is everything okay?'

'Why must you think something's wrong every time I phone?' Juno joked. 'But in truth, I have just been in touch with palace security.'

'Oh? Why?'

'You need to go to the Rose Room now,' Juno said.

'Why?' Jade hated the Rose Room.

'I haven't time to explain, but trust me, Jade. Go there now.'

Her sister ended the call before Jade could ask anything more.

She didn't want to go. She hadn't even had the chance to get changed. Feeling a little sorry for herself, she hoped it wasn't Juno's idea of something fun. She wanted to curl in a ball, cuddle a hot-water bottle and hide.

Step. Up. You're the freaking Queen of Monrova.

Alvaro Byrne had to admit, he was intimidated as hell. And damn if he didn't feel sorry for Jade right now. The palace was stunning but definitely designed to awe and humble the average person and this room was the worst. It looked like something from a movie set in medieval times—a throne on a dais, dust motes hanging in the gloom, despite those magnificent stained-glass windows. All it needed was an executioner in a suit of armour waiting with his axe…or maybe that was just how Alvaro was feeling on the inside. As if he were about to beg for mercy—plead for his life, from the most powerful person he'd encountered. And that wasn't anything to do with her crown.

He'd been unable to admit it—not for days and least of all to himself. He'd thought he was invincible—that he had everything he wanted and needed and was happy enough. But the happiness he'd felt in those few days with her?

Whole. Other. Level.

He'd tried to blame it on euphoria—on an ephemeral spell of sex and hormones.

Bull. Shit.

The soul-destroying gap in his heart—in his life—as she'd walked out, taking away the one thing he'd wanted most of all before he'd even registered how desperately he needed and wanted and, yes, loved her.

Today he'd watched her on her walkabout from across the road, leaning against the corner of a building at a safe, unrecognisable distance. The crowds had been huge and had rushed that flimsy-looking fence when she'd appeared. But they'd been respectful. She'd taken her time—shared smiles and said how delighted and excited she was for her sister. Easily sidestepping questions about what she'd done in Manhattan during her switch. She'd managed to avoid any mention of him and he'd convinced his staff to say nothing about 'PJ' to the press. To his pleasure, they'd all agreed. And he knew it wasn't to please him, it was to support her. In such a short time she'd earned their respect and loyalty—and yes, their sense of protectiveness.

He'd got the same vibe from the throngs gathered here. Watching her on the walkabout, he'd decided it was because of the quiet kindness that was somehow so obvious, despite her restrained, almost demure appearance. She'd looked beautiful in a long-sleeved, pretty-patterned winter gown in green, a short cape keeping her shoulders warm. She'd had no problems in high-heeled boots on those old cobblestones. Her hair was half up, half down, intricately entwined somehow in that gleaming diamond tiara with its trio of emeralds. She couldn't have looked more picture-perfect regal—graceful and elegant, dignified and remote. Yet those eyes of hers had been so filled with emotion. She was, he knew, so very human.

He also knew he wasn't worthy of her. But he couldn't stay away. He couldn't stop himself from being selfish. Only she'd say he wasn't, she'd say he *deserved* it—happiness. Well, so did she.

The double doors suddenly swung inward, two liveried footmen attending each. Alvaro braced. Nothing like a dramatic opening. He stood where he was, in the centre of that vast room, as the Queen of Monrova walked in.

The doors sealed shut behind her. The quiet thud of their closure reverberated around the room. The Queen stopped just inside the room and stared at him.

She didn't smile, instead she turned paler and paler.

'Jade—' He broke off as she flinched.

Every muscle chilled and he couldn't move. But she visibly pulled herself together.

'Alvaro.'

Hearing his name on her lips jump-started his brain.

'Getting into this palace is a challenge,' he said. 'I tried to phone you. I got Juno instead. But she was helpful.'

'Why are you here?'

He half smiled; she had a good brain. But sometimes, even good brains couldn't figure out the blindingly obvious right away—especially when there was fear involved. He knew that one personally. Fear stopped normal function. Fear made people freeze. And she'd frozen right now—just as he had. But he was breathing again. And he could win this. Yet suddenly another emotion rose in him—and it wasn't the one it ought to have been. It was anger.

'You think it's okay to tell someone you love them and then just walk away? Walk out with no intention of ever returning? Ever getting in touch again? Of leaving for *life*?'

Jade's heart thundered at his sudden flare. She was still grasping the fact that he was here—that somehow her inner radar had got it right. And he'd come to...*yell* at her? Absurdly, that didn't upset her, because she was suddenly too furious herself.

'I thought that's what you wanted,' she snapped back at him.

'You didn't give me a second to know what I wanted.'

'You didn't know already?'

The banked heat in his gaze exploded. 'You didn't even try to fight. For the last few days...' He dragged in a breath, visibly trying to calm down. 'I've been so angry. Too furious to think straight. But then the fury died and I was left in hell.' He shook his head and slowed himself down. 'It was only then that I began to think.'

Jade stared at him, her own fury evaporating as swiftly as it had risen.

'And I realised you did fight. Just by telling me how you felt about...' He trailed off, his expression softening. 'That was you fighting. Speaking up? That's big for anyone, and huge for you. But I said nothing. I'm sorry, Jade. I was so stunned— not just by what you said, but by you. And I was so scared I couldn't think. Even when, yes, I knew the answer already. It terrified me.'

Her chest tightened under strain, as if her ribs were shrinking or her heart were getting bigger.

'Do you know, it's so damn hard to get anywhere near you? You say I'm isolated—some people might think this is a *prison*.'

'It's my home,' she said, fierce pride enveloping her. 'It's not a prison to me.'

'No.' He nodded. 'I watched you today, and this is where you belong. You shine everywhere, Jade. But most of all, here.' He stepped closer. 'And it's why you left me, isn't it? Because you thought there was no way this could work out.'

Her poor heart broke all over again. Because that was true.

'But you can't give something like that only to then take it away again.' He actually waggled his finger at her.

'I wanted to leave it with you. I wanted you to treasure it.'

'So you didn't mean it?'

She drew breath to stave off the sharp stab of pain. He took advantage of the second to step closer still, only he was smiling.

'Do you think you could give me a second chance, Jade?'

Of course. Always.

But her only response was to tremble.

'The problem is,' he explained quietly, '*that* memory isn't enough for me. I want more. I want to wake up with you every morning and to go to bed with you every night. I want to have as many moments of as many days together as we can. I don't want us to be apart, Jade. You know why.' He finally reached her, finally put his hands on her waist, grounding her here in reality to hear him. 'Because I love you.'

All she could do was blink, trying to clear the blurring tears so she could see properly…because she was trying to *believe*?

His lips twisted. 'It's hard to trust, isn't it?' He lifted his hand to touch her hair. 'Hard to believe that someone might accept you, want you, love you…just for you, just as you are. That even if you have nothing, were no one, even if you didn't do the things expected of you…that you would still be loved. I didn't just find it hard to believe that someone could feel that for me, it was impossible. That's my problem. Believing. Trusting. Even though it's the thing I want more than anything else in the world, from the person I want more in the world. I'm sorry I let you go. I'm sorry I let you down. I'm sorry you ran so quickly before I could think. But I've done nothing except think since. And do you know what I've realised?'

Impossibly overwhelmed, she shook her head.

'Wanting love. Wanting fun, friendship, laughter and, of course, fantastic sex…all those things shouldn't be out of the ordinary for anyone. It shouldn't just be a "treat day" thing. And we shouldn't have to feel excessively grateful for getting something we *all* should have. We all deserve.' His hands tightened on her waist—energy passing through his skin to her. 'It's too close to feeling *guilty*, Jade. As if we don't deserve it in some way. As if we should feel grateful for crumbs… I want the whole damn cake. Why shouldn't any of us get a cake? Jade, you should have a cake. So should I.' He lifted one hand and cupped her face with his big strong palm. 'I love you. Every beautiful thing about you. What do you say, sweetheart?' He brushed away her tear with his thumb. 'Say something. Anything.'

'I love you too.'

His smile was slow and still nervous and so heartfelt. 'I was really hoping you'd say that.'

The skim of his lips over hers was like a gossamer graze. The gentlest gift—not *tentative*, but as if he too were still slightly wary of believing this was real. Like a swimmer dipping only a toe in the water rather than diving straight in, in case the depth was deceptive. She kissed him back as softly—it was so rare, this connection. And then the emotion overwhelmed her so much she shuddered—she'd missed him so much. And then his arms were tight and his mouth hungry and the kiss was everything—all the passion absolving all the absence and her heart soared.

He released her suddenly, breathless and hoarse. 'I have something for you.'

Her heart thundered as he put his hand in his pocket. His smile curved as he pulled his fist out. She knew he held something small and suddenly everything was moving too quickly.

'Alvaro—'

He flipped his hand and unfurled his fingers so she could see what sat in his palm. A metal ring, yes. But it was a key ring. A single house key was attached, together with a silver charm of a little lighthouse. She instantly understood that it was a key to his cottage. He wanted to share his sanctuary with her.

'You can go there any time,' he muttered, still

breathless. 'I'll always meet you. I'll always share everything I have with you.'

Her heart melted but at the same time an agony of uncertainty slammed into her. *How* was this going to work? 'I want this. I want you. But...'

'You're worried about protocol? Because I'm not a prince?'

'You're a prince to *me*,' she said sadly. 'But you don't understand what this world is like.'

'That's true.' He laughed as he looked around the stuffily ornate room. 'But I'll learn.'

'You need time.' She felt terrified. What if he hated it? What if—?

'*I* don't need time, sweetheart, but I understand that you do.' He cupped her face again. 'We'll take it slow.'

How could there possibly be slow? Once people—the world—found out she was in a relationship, the pressures that would come on them would be immense.

'You live on the other side of the Atlantic,' she fretted. 'You run a massive company that's been your life... I can't ask you to give that all up.'

'Do I have to give it up?' Smiling gently, he slowly shook his head.

'The politics and business...' she muttered. 'It gets complicated.'

That soft amusement in his eyes deepened. 'Do you know what I do, Jade?'

'Buy companies. Develop them.'

'Actually, mostly I just problem-solve. I like complicated. I like challenge. And you problem-solve too. You're good at it.'

But there were problems, and there were *problems*. And surely this was impossible. 'I can't ask you to move here.' She shook her head sadly. 'I won't ask that of you. It won't work. It won't last.'

'You're thinking of your parents.' He put his broad palm on her spine and drew her to rest against him. He was her tower of strength. 'I know you've been stuck in your palace a bit, darling, but times have changed, and technology with it. If I can work from my lighthouse, I can work from here when we're ready.'

She wanted to believe him so very much.

'But it worries me that they're going to hound you. So what if we steal some more time together before anyone has to find out about us?'

Her heart fluttered and she lifted her head to look into his eyes—warm amber shone at her. 'You want to be my secret boyfriend?'

'Desperately.'

'I want you to myself.' Just for a while. And then? Excitement suddenly poured through her body as she suddenly realised this was all real. All true. 'I want you for ever,' she confessed. 'So much.'

His expression lit up. 'Well, why don't you show me your secret passages, then, my lady?'

With a giggle, she grasped his hand. 'You'll have to follow me.'

His fingers curled tight around hers. 'Gladly.'

She led him along the still, quiet corridor to her private apartment.

'Oh, this is…better.' He glanced around her lounge.

'I've ordered new cushions,' she assured him.

'Fantastic.' He laughed and hauled her into his arms. 'I can be patient, Jade.'

But his hands and body said the absolute opposite. Jade simply swooned against him.

'We'll do the proper protocol,' he promised. 'Whatever your palace people want, but only when *you* want, your timeline, sweetheart. Because you're worth waiting for and this is your call. Whenever, however, this has to be, then I'll be here. I'm all in.'

'You don't mind all the hoops?' Her eyes filled again as he moved against her with such powerful passion. 'There'll be so many hoops.'

'As long as you don't mind stealing away to the lighthouse with me sometimes,' he whispered, his breath lost. 'That's my wish.'

'Mine too.' She shuddered. 'I would love that. Because I love you.'

She moved with him, their breathing aligned, their hearts beating in time.

He held her close and tight, the way she loved, and his smile, his love, shone down on her.

'Then that's what we'll do.'

CHAPTER FIFTEEN

New Year's Day, one year later

JADE GENTLY SQUEEZED Alvaro's hand twice as they stepped away from the woman and young child—their pre-agreed wordless signal that she was finally ready to finish. This walkabout had taken even longer than last year's, but Juno and King Leonardo had arrived from Severene to attend as a special surprise. The crowds had roared ecstatically, constantly calling questions to the couple about their sweet daughter, Alice, currently fast asleep in Monrova palace.

The second they were back within the palace walls, Leonardo wrapped his arm around his wife's waist to bring her closer. Watching, Jade melted inside. She'd never seen Juno so happy, nor Leonardo so demonstrative. He visibly adored his wife and child and it filled Jade with such satisfaction.

She glanced up and saw Alvaro's gaze on her—his smile tender and teasing and so knowing.

She smiled back. 'I'm happy for her.'

'I know.' This time his hand tightened on hers. 'It's time for us to refuel, yes? Because that took longer than anyone was expecting, right?'

Well, that was because everyone had wanted to see *him*. After getting over their delight at seeing Juno and Leonardo, the crowds had been momentarily stunned to see Alvaro step forward beside Jade. Until today he'd hung back at official events, happy to accompany her but remain 'in the shadows', as he'd put it. As if he ever could be anything like invisible. And for ages now, the public had been asking to see and hear more from him. So she'd been thrilled when he'd agreed to join her today.

They'd had almost six months to themselves at first. Stealing away, solidifying that passion and playfulness that had sparked from the moment they'd met. Then, of course, the press had found out. Alvaro had begun visiting Monrova 'officially' and eventually 'palace sources' had confirmed he was the Queen's consort. Another six months later, he'd been proven right again as they'd problem-solved their way through constitutional traditions, so now it was accepted that he was with her here in Monrova more often than he wasn't.

But they'd gone to the States for Christmas. In early December they'd invited Ellen to visit Monrova and attend the Winter Ball as Jade's special guest. It had been the best ball ever because of that, in Jade's opinion. Then Jade and Alvaro had accompanied Ellen home and actually stayed at her house for Christmas dinner for the first time—with Alvaro's special butter and no work whatsoever. Then the two of them had headed to the lighthouse for their own private Christmas night.

Now Jade glanced at the dining table in her private apartment and turned to Alvaro. 'What's this?'

'Just a little something delicious.' He shrugged carelessly, but the warmth in his gaze was a total giveaway.

The chocolate cake was glazed in a shiny, rich ganache and looked so gorgeously lickable that it gave Jade a few ideas. 'It's not my birthday,' she teased with a slow blink.

'Can we only enjoy cake on special occasions?' he asked, just as sweetly innocent.

Her smile turned a little wicked and her mouth watered. Jade picked up the knife. The cake looked dreamily indulgent, but as she cut into it the blade skimmed over something hard in the centre. She shot Alvaro a suspicious glance. He merely raised his eyebrows.

She tried again and this time, when she removed a wedge, she discovered not a cascade of candy inside, but that a small box sat in a hidden centre cavity.

She stared for a split second, then her heart sprinted and her lungs tightened. Because she knew what was going to be in that box. She had to drop the knife on the table because her fingers were suddenly nerveless.

'Jade?'

Her eyes were already watering.

He reached out and took her hands, turning her to face him. 'Marry me,' he said simply. 'Be my queen.'

Exhilaration flooded her even as those tears trickled.

'Does this really come as a surprise to you, sweetheart?' He softly wiped the tears before gently kissing her. There was such promise and such truth in that kiss.

She drew a shuddering breath and pressed closer, overwhelmed with longing and an urgent need to love him completely. It was her only possible answer at that point.

He rapidly shifted, understanding her need as always. In record speed he got her on the sofa—and as searing need stormed through her he caressed her, as unleashed as her in moments.

'I've got you.' He held her tightly and kissed her burning skin. 'I'm here.'

And he was—with her, around her, in her, not just her anchor but her lighthouse—protecting her, here for her. And as he enveloped her with his strength and size, she couldn't hold him tightly enough. He was her everything and he gave her everything—all of himself. She arched to meet him, straining to gift him the same, until she could no longer contain anything and she crumpled completely in an explosion of love.

When she could finally open her eyes, his lips curved in a twist of that old arrogance. 'Aren't you ever going to answer me?' he teased as he gazed into her soul. 'I've been patient so very long…'

She smiled—as if she hadn't answered him already? But she knew that he needed words as much as he needed touch and action, just as she did. And, as always, he was impossible to deny.

'Yes,' she breathed as her heart burst with fullness. 'Always and for ever, *yes*.'

* * * * *

Blown away by
The Queen's Impossible Boss?
*Discover the previous instalment in
the Christmas Princess Swap duet*
The Royal Pregnancy Test *by Heidi Rice.*

*And why not explore these other
Natalie Anderson stories?*

Secrets Made in Paradise
Shy Queen in the Royal Spotlight
The Greek's One-Night Heir
The Innocent's Emergency Wedding

Available now!